SILENT CAULDRON

E. B. Moore

Frayed Edge Press
Philadelphia, PA

Published by Frayed Edge Press in 2025

Frayed Edge Press
Philadelphia, PA 19101

http://frayededgepress.com

Cover photo by Dr. Sandra Trappen
Cover design by E.B. Moore

Library of Congress Control Number: 2025936583

Publishers Cataloging-in-Publication Data

Names: Moore, E.B.
Title: Silent cauldron / E. B. Moore.
Description: Philadelphia, PA : Frayed Edge Press, 2025.
Identifiers: LCCN 2025936583 | ISBN 9781642510645 (pbk.) | ISBN
    9781642510676 (EPUB) | ISBN 9781642510669 (Kindle)
Subjects: LCSH: Women prisoners -- Fiction. | Prisons -- Pennsylvania -- 19th
    century -- Fiction. | Cross-dressers -- Fiction. | Quakers -- Fiction. | BISAC:
    FICTION / Historical / 19th Century / General. | FICTION / Psychological.
    | FICTION / Women.
Classification: LCC PS3563.O674 S55 2025 | DDC 813 M--dc22
LC record available at https://lccn.loc.gov/2025936583

DEDICATION

For my children, a prayer
that they may know the balm
of silence

but beware

this same silence
honed to a blade and ceiling hung
Oh pendulous sword

"A woman should learn in quietness and full submission."
Timothy 2:1

"Can such things happen and be done with…"
Journey into the Whirlwind
Eugenia Semyonovna Ginzburg

PART I

SOLITARY

EASTERN STATE PENITENTIARY

Inside amorphous years no star
to plot a course, no melt of dawn
no sun dials the hour—

CHAPTER 1

WILLA

In this silence, I am footsteps. I am the hand on Six's shoulder. She calls me Willa. Friend. Confidant risen from deep underground.

To her ear, I am the sound in soundlessness.

I am communion in her solitary cell. Vision when she is blind. Witness where she won't look.

And I am the storehouse of what once was hers—times when she was Samanthos, a girl called Sam, after her grandfather; Anthos, she being the flower of her parents' latter years, their unexpected blessing. At first.

A blessing before their girl wore britches. She insisted. A blessing before their girl, mistaken for a boy, stepped "out of order."

Thrilled to be so mistaken, she dared breach the world reserved for men where women were silent and money spoke. Where power overrode the rational.

Whispering in her lonely ear, I reiterate those years, the happy and the fraught, that led to this forever of being Number Six. She told of those times so often I feel we lived them together— Sam's memories mine. We two as one, even before I became her shield.

Yet in this cell, she scrubs her mind of tortures I can't erase. Every prod, her every penetration carried as my own.

Though I am her soother, I now find myself kneeling close at her ear, Six sprawled on the granite floor. Blood streaks the whitewashed wall. Blood on the floor, and the fault is mine.

"Six." I grip her shoulder, shake her. "Escape. For Lord-sake, we must."

So much suffering—could it be for naught, her very life squandered? "Up." I hammer her.

No more cajoling. No more pretty picturings of cream that could never rise in this curdled existence. She knows there's no milk here, much less cream. Cream is not for the likes of us, that buttery promise left distant as planets.

Once, she'd imagined other planets. Now she's fallen through a fissure in this one, wandering to forget the now even as we live it.

Her eyes droop. "Leave me be."

Pain curls her, tight and tighter, as if she clutches a treasure I'd steal. I rub the back of her neck. We in this dim chamber must care, one for the other. And I do. I care. Mostly. Though there be times I'd happily kick her backside. And now, I've done worse.

"Up." Survival's in her. "Up, or they'll dance on your grave."

Barth Kane and his father. I dangle the blackguards before her the way I'd shake carrots at a weary horse. She must fight.

My Samanthos, Quaker to the bone. Vengeance is not hers, nor violence, but resist she must. Sam, the child who wouldn't stomp a beetle, yet refused to wear frocks and donned her brother's out-grown britches.

Those days, she'd proved a scrapper, availing herself of a burgeoning world. Resistance worth the risk.

Worth the risk until they tore a hole in her world.

Worth the risk until, "Rape." Sam accused, arrested. Not Barth.

Logic in the wind—a bird, feathers a-flap, caught in a gyre and swallowed. As was Sam. As was Anna, Sam's one true friend and witness.

The two of them, each the holder of what the other kept hidden—private happenings bound in solemn promise. Say nary a word—their lives in the balance.

I lift Six by her jacket. Her head lolls against my legs, blood on my pants, on my hands. So much blood. "Up now."

Her eyes narrow slits, she mumbles, "Willa...leave me... to my trees." She clings to the Cherry Hill of old, its orchard full of spring flowers turned fruitful by fall.

Holding fast, she travels back to those days before reformers felled the trees, tore roots from the earth; before they massed this gravid hive of buzzing silence where we've stayed entombed in stone all these untold years.

"No, Six. Another hour, and we're both dead."

PART II

AS IT WAS IN THE BEGINNING

Silence, the healer—Silence, a sword

When she told me, "Oh Willa, they lie," how I wished I'd been beside her back then, we two standing as one. Unhidden. Our voice loud.

CHAPTER 2

ROAD TO CHERRY HILL

1833

Sam once ripe with promise, a gleaner of books, worlds knocking at her door. How now Six with this bitter harvest—

Morning warmth eased into the blister of an August afternoon as a one-horse cart jolted toward Cherry Hill: the constable's name for Sam's destination. She balanced on the plank seat, calloused hands bound behind her, and listened to the high cry of cicadas.

They coursed through hedgerow trees and soared over fields, wheat seeds nodding while strident songs arced and dropped until drowned beneath the iron-wheeled crush on gravel.

A welcome breeze lifted strands of dark hair stuck to the sweat on her neck, hairs fraying from the single braid down her back. No matter how sultry the day, this fresh air offered relief from the village lockup and its cauldron of drunks.

If she couldn't be free, at least the time ahead, solitary in a cell, seemed the most she could hope for—a blessing after three weeks of her town's lockup. Oh, the cacophony. It had her holding her ears, her eyes watchful for the next loose fist coming her way.

Silence—she looked forward to it. Silence would restore her, as it did at Quaker Meeting. As it did in the fields with only the whisper of insects.

In lockup, what little sleep she managed found her slumped on a bench or stretched out on boards, if other prisoners had returned to their lives. They often left a generous gift of fleas, keeping her awake with incessant itch.

She longed for what couldn't be: her vision of university, being a writer, a professor, a poet. The possibilities endless.

Not even her studies, the quiet evenings reading at home, could be hers. She'd treasured those times in the family cottage. Now gone, those hours close with Father and his books, lessons with her brother Paul. Even Mamma's life didn't look so confining—Mamma in her rocker, gray streaked hair, cheeks hollow. Mamma, at the end of summer days in the garden, rocking on the porch, in her lap a bowl of peas she thumbed from their shells. Or else shucking corn, the husks piled at her feet.

Though Mamma knew how, nary a word would she read from a book. Her hours were restricted to toil prescribed by the past, by strictures long-dead men deemed appropriate.

What did these men know of Sam? Of her capabilities? Her curiosity?

In winter, Mamma sat by the fire. She knitted sweaters, darned socks, sewed patches, and when absolutely necessary, made a new garment.

What danger could there be in books? A thing hazardous for women, but not for men? What danger was there in Sam wearing britches? What danger in working at a stable beyond her own farm?

Sam couldn't accept Mamma's drab habit. She wouldn't. The last frock Mamma made for Sam still hung on a hook back home in the bedroom closet, a constant reminder of Mamma's dashed hopes for Sam's marriage. For grandchildren to come.

Sam: an ever-present disappointment. No one knew then how far beyond disappointment Sam would fall.

All her farm days, she'd reveled in the whispered-drops of passing showers, and once the rain had passed, she, her brother, and parents watched the sun drift behind lacey canopies. And this past summer, Sam had looked forward to autumn, to the harvest safely in, the elms reaching red to the clouds. These sights of autumn were no longer hers to see or smell. Not this one. Not any to come.

Relaxed and careless in her love of learning and the land, she'd taken family times for granted. She never suspected that her world would do less than age with the seasons and be reborn come spring, a promise the land never broke. She trusted the land.

But people—she'd been slow to learn. People were different.

At least in the cell, according to the prison founders, people wouldn't be a problem. She'd be alone.

Sway-backed and boney, the horse plodded one curve to the next, the dirt track rife with stones unearthed after washout. The cart's relentless wheels ground onward, and Sam, fighting the pitch and yaw, clung to the bench, her balance more demanding than riding Father's velocipede.

She wedged one leg under the seat. Her britches dug into the soft skin behind her knee, circulation cut until one foot lost feeling and she traded legs, tucking the other one under. Two working legs and fortunate to have them, she told herself, as blood needled her toes.

Now, bound for Cherry Hill, she remembered this road and the orchard as it had been when she and Father, on horseback, headed for a visit with friends from his old life. University life in Philadelphia, before they moved to their very own cottage, with a barn and fields surrounded by woods, with no neighbors close. Quiet, an isolated life where Father lived in a sphere above everyday toil, not fitting in with sharecroppers or Chesterton, the owner of Meadowvale, with the stable where Paul held sway.

In spring Father and Sam had ridden, early morning into mid-afternoon, past woods and fields into a still orchard where bees hummed, their legs heavy with sweet collection. Trees, never to bloom again, had been sacrificed for a more silent quiet.

On city visits, Sam had quailed at the scurry and shout and yet was thrilled to enter thought-filled chambers where she listened from a corner, content as professors debated deforestation, the fate of the red man, freedom for the negro. And deeper still, the power of God, how it fueled a better world.

Or was it money, scything a swath through the unwary? Yes, the power of money—and she'd seen it for real.

Closer to her heart, it had rankled her when professors, all men, laughed and dismissed the suggestion that women might ponder important matters. Sam shrank in her corner, extinguishing any hint of the feminine.

If entering the work of a greater world was what she wanted—and she wanted it more than anything—then her identity must remain hidden. Intentionally hidden.

"Intentionality," Mamma had said, "makes you a liar." What did Mamma know? A sharp-faced woman of many Godly opinions, she didn't want to see beyond their fence. The safety. The sanctity of home. Sam kept herself to herself and prayed no one would ask. She couldn't outright lie. She wouldn't.

Fascinated yet frightened, that secret had nagged at her. Sometimes she wished she hadn't gone with Father.

Now, she wished that she could stay forever in some peaceful orchard. But they'd razed every tree, every blade of grass.

Even now bound for Cherry Hill, riding the wood bench, ropes burning her wrists with every lurch—the cart, no doubt, fit with square wheels—she couldn't believe what Mamma believed: that Sam had no right to an expanding world.

"There she be," the driver said, part chuckle, part awe.

Sam lifted her eyes from the road and looked over the top of her wire-rimmed glasses. She'd been bracing for jolts to come and hadn't tracked the horizon, didn't see the edifice rise until it filled the evening sky, stone on stone, the crenelated towers stark and looming above the denuded plain.

Living at the other end of the county, she'd heard of plans for housing criminals, a kinder incarceration, a place aimed at redemption. Quaker inspired, this served as a replacement for prisons like Auburn where miscreants mixed with capital offenders, where young ones learned the tools of criminal trades instead of rejecting felonious habits.

This new edifice—calling it Cherry Hill fit their benign intentions—would be the antidote to tortures of old. It was built in eighteen-twenty-nine and now, into the thirties, the penitentiary held a few women as well as men. An odd kind of equality.

Behind the battlements, these Quakers planned solitary cells, windowless places to contemplate and repent under a skylight. "The eye of God." A place where offenders would become an asset to society. A fine intention.

After the town's holding-cell, yes, Sam welcomed their notion. She understood how a peaceful place to reflect could work. But now, seeing the broken earth, the granite block plantings, the chambered fortress full-grown, her notions of this place of penance faltered.

The driver reined in his horse and they waited, dwarfed at the base of the great façade. The horse drooped his head low before doors—those doors wider than five oaks put together, planks shot with iron rivets. The doors swung open into a dark maw. The driver clicked his tongue, and the reluctant horse leaned on leather traces, passing from light into deep shadow.

Grit-filled hinges shrieked. The doors slowly closed. Shadow swallowed the horse, cart, driver, and Sam. She winced.

"Intentional," the driver said. "A hint of what comes." And so saying, he stood close and drew a coarse hood over Sam's head, shutting out the bowel they'd entered. She gasped.

The hood mashed her glasses, metal frame biting the bridge of her nose as the cloth closed on her own quickened breath. "Hey, wai…"

Something smacked Sam's elbow. "Stand."

On shaky legs, her hands still tied at her back, she stood, knees bent. Every nervous breath pulled at stale cloth. She shifted her footing, a fruitless attempt at balance, and out from beneath her the cart melted. Between her world and the next she hung timeless until instinct tucked her head, rounded her shoulders, ready for the coming earth—but the bonds allowed her too little bend.

This wasn't like falling off a horse, the speed judged, earth where she knew it would be, the roll anticipated and attained in one smooth motion bringing her back to her feet. No. This time, all-too-solid earth hit the whole of her side, knocking wind from her innards. The hood ballooned. She couldn't pull another breath.

From above, a new voice, "Say nothing."

Sam flopped, a waterless fish, gills spread. They clamped shut. Spread again. She couldn't talk even if she wanted to.

Pain subsiding, her breath began again in sips.

"Well, well, what have we here?" said a man, his voice higher than Sam's.

"All yours, Fergus," the driver said. "Your friend Kane sends greetings. 'Special care,' he says. 'No repentance, no release, and you could be warden.'"

A gleeful laugh. "Me, warden!"

Kane—ubiquitous as the fleas Sam couldn't scratch. Only God knew what special care would mean.

She couldn't see the cart and horse retreat—could only hear the clopping hooves, the creak of closing doors. Their final boom echoed off stone.

By one bound arm, Fergus, she supposed, lifted Sam to her feet. Pain shot through her shoulders as he ushered her through a doorway into the sound of running water.

CHAPTER 3

PROCESSING

Stripped of Sam

An arm blocked her chest, and she heard the whisper of steel against leather—a knife drawn from its sheath, an everyday event in her life at the stable, but here…she froze.

Steel slid cold on her veined wrist; skin pinched. She twisted sideways.

"You want a slit wrist?" He drew the sharp edge against the rope and sawed strand by strand until Sam's shoulders loosened.

Her arms, how they longed to hang free at her side; but as the ropes fell, her limbs did not. She bent double, the pain of freedom sharper than being bound.

In the dark, she stumbled against him. "Please…"

He caught her upper arm. More pain kept her on her feet. "From here on," he said, "silence."

Silence she could do, and common sense said to keep so, though common sense hadn't applied since her arrest. *Hers*, when it should have been Barth for what he'd done.

At trial, Sam wanted to explain. It hadn't been mayhem and certainly not attempted murder. But no. "Just 'Yes' or 'No.' The deed, did you do it?" Nothing more wanted.

"Did you? Did you?" Yes, but not as presented, truth twisted on their tongues.

Anger rose as it had in the courtroom. Renewed breath bounced off the bag over her head.

Had she tried to kill Barth? Wanted to…?

It all happened so fast. Stopping Barth, driving him away from herself and Anna, driving him from the stable—that intent had swamped her. Nothing else mattered. Her previous animosity had nothing to do with it.

And Barth? What of his want, and the want Sam once had for him? This, a piece of herself she'd rather not touch. Still immersed in confusion, she shied from his want and hers.

Shied, as she did now from the hand yanking the hood. It came off along with bits of hair, and worse… "My glasses!" They flew.

Sam lunged, fingers spread. A foot hooked her ankle. She sprawled, palms out, the heels of her hands scraping as the glasses skidded from reach.

On her belly, she stayed still. The man circled her, his skinny legs and boots all she could see. Those boots, cat quiet, the leather covered in socks. Who wears socks over boots?

She twisted her head, the rest of him coming in view: sharp face, one eye in a suspicious squint. The sly lift of his lip opened to yellowed, rat-like teeth.

She tried to rise. He planted a boot on the small of her back, using her the way he would a footstool.

"I need…" She choked.

He leaned, grinding her hipbones to the stone. Another person coughed.

Sam peered up. A second man waited by the door, thick of neck, broad in the shoulders. His ample girth filled the frame where he waited, head stooped. Subservient.

"Come on, Wee-Ned, don't be shy," said the high voice of Fergus. "Gimp yourself over here."

She could see nothing wee about him, but the face round and more red-cheeked by the second looked boyish. His boots were also covered in socks. One leg shorter than the other made him limp. The socks whispered him across the floor where he stood next to Sam's rump.

Rat-Face lifted his boot. "Come on, Wee-One, you know the drill."

Not-so-wee-Ned tapped her side with his toe. "Up," he said without conviction. "Hair first, on the bench."

Up, she understood, and climbed on stinging hands and knees. The sting hurried her. On her feet, hair was another matter. She didn't dare ask.

"Move." Rat-Face seized the braid at her back. He tugged her to a bench against the wall, shoved down on her stiffened shoulders. She perched.

Ned passed him a set of shears, the kind Sam had used on the family sheep. Shearing was a spring job, but she wasn't his sheep. She wouldn't be.

"Don't move." Close to her nose, he snick-snicked the blades together. He jerked the braid and, keeping it taught, set the blades against the roots and cut in small grinding increments, hacking and hacking until the shears snapped shut on the last strands, the braid left hanging limp as a dead squirrel in his upraised fist.

"Hey, Gimp." He threw the braid at Ned. "Want a keepsake?" Ned jumped, hands above his head.

"What a girly-boy." Rat-Face laughed. "You don't want fleas?"

Pulling a fistful of shortened hair, he tipped her head and with careless speed sheared around it, gouging her scalp when she twitched.

The short hairs fell in her collar, over her shoulders, and into her lap. With the final fistful shorn, near bald, her head felt the cold like a breeze from an open window. There were no windows.

"Stand."

She did and brushed the loose hair prickling her neck.

"Don't bother." Ned prodded her to the room's center. "Strip."

Which was it: not to bother, or to strip the rest of the hair from her clothes? This was a willful misinterpretation. She wasn't about to strip.

"Now!" Rat-Face shoved her. She fell on her rump, hands down, jolting her shoulders. "Everything off."

For a moment, shock blocked her.

"Move," growled Rat-Face, his irritation smoldering.

Everything off? Surely not everything. A chill puckered her skin.

She sat on the floor, shoulders hunched, legs crossed. No one, not even Mamma, had seen her naked for years—not since she could bathe herself.

In lockup with no bath to be had, she'd been in the same clothes all three weeks. Most crimes kept people only overnight. Lock-up wasn't equipped for more, yet an attempted killing demanded more.

Mostly, she hadn't thought of her body. She left assumptions to others and gladly left the wrong impressions uncorrected. Armed with this mistaken notion, she'd stepped beyond her mother's confinements, and used her body like a tool, muscles honed to achievements beyond what seemed possible for the weaker sex. Being a boy broke wide the possibilities: not just the physical world but a world of knowledge, a universe not available to girls, as if females were of weaker mind too.

What made men of old think they knew of her capabilities? Or men of now, for that matter. She wouldn't have it. She had ventured through a door into new possibilities until the opening closed, slamming her fingers. Slamming her toes; toes on feet too large to be graceful.

Sam bent her bare head. Elbows tight to her side, she looked at the worn weave of her shirt, hillocks beneath so minor they didn't show. Buttons disappeared below the beltline, her breeches loose over nonexistent hips, her sinuous legs. She couldn't move.

With a twist from behind, her shirt tightened to her collarbones. Her head stayed bent. What had she expected?

Within seconds, buttons popped. A knee in her back pitched her full-length on the floor, and with cloth ripping, they rolled her until she splayed, spine to cold granite, naked but for socks. These were taken last.

Ned lurched a step back, palms up. "Whoooa!" he said under his breath. "Fergus, he's a girl!"

"You noticed!" Rat-Face poked him in the ear. "Six women here on the Hill, and this one's mine. Special treatment."

Ned, with a hesitant smile, tracked the whole of Sam's body. "Yeah? And what'll the warden say?"

"He don't have to know. And you... hands off."

Good God.

Ned took another retreating step. Cheeks a-flame, he looked at the floor.

Sam shivered. Lying on her side, she curled her chest inward; her back curved to an insubstantial shell.

Arms crossed on stiff nipples, her skin went bumpy as fingers of cold air touched places never left uncovered. She closed her eyes against the windowless room.

Did she think herself invisible? As if four years old, believing if she didn't see the men, they wouldn't see her? That the stone enclosure wouldn't exist? Oh, how she wished it. To be four again. To believe.

Efforts not entirely in vain, darkness hid the men. This way, she didn't have to see Ned's mortal embarrassment, though she heard a quickened breath. Smelled his sweat.

"Bath," said Rat-Face, his indifference reassuring. Then to Ned, "Your turn."

From the floor Sam, eyes open, saw a block and tackle waiting, the rope cleated. Blocks dangled at the ceiling. She craned her neck. The hoist hung above an open tank big enough to scald a hog. She shivered.

For pigs. Surely, not her tub.

I'm not a hog. Not a hog—almost a prayer.

They wouldn't scald her, wouldn't scrape her remaining bristles. She wasn't going to be eaten. Fleas only.

Think pork. It made sense for a prison. The animals: garbage fed, no grain needed, no grazing, ten to a litter twice a year. She knew pigs. They grew huge. She'd raised them. Slaughtered and scalded them.

Her first exposure came when she turned three. "Old enough to prance about, is old enough to work," Mamma had scolded.

Sam, with a bucket of slops, crossed the porch and trudged down the path to the pigpen. Against November's nip, she held her shawl close, kicking at long skirts. How did Mamma manage?

At the rail fence, she lifted her bucket. The slops would need to be dumped past Delilah and her four shoats as they crowded the fence, snouts raised to the odorous feast. She climbed the rails and caught her skirt as she balanced, stomach over the top.

Both hands on the bucket handle, she stretched, arms extended. Her skirt loosened and her body pitched forward, dumping the bucket, herself, a scatter of peelings, eggshells, and chicken heads, into the muck. This muck easily washed. She'd come to treasure this filth. Her body left untarnished.

"It's full." Ned, at the opposite wall, turned off the water running into a metal tub that Sam hadn't noticed. Thank God, yes, the tank for pigs.

"Up," said Ned, focusing somewhere east of her head.

She stood, keeping her back to him, hands shielding her private hair, and sidled toward the tub. Its claw feet flexed on the floor as if, given leave, it would run.

Her toes curled. She braced her arms on the tub's rounded edge and eyed the ring-on-crusted-ring within. Its lines boasted the tub's history much as a tree marks its years.

"No lolling," said Ned, imploring more than directing. He shuffled close behind her. "In."

She swung one foot up sideways, an attempt at stepping in without spreading her knees, when a smack on the buttock launched her.

"Wash," said Rat-Face; a command.

Chill and gray, the water rose to the top ring as her backside, then belly, then chest submerged.

Ned gave her a rag and a block of brown soap. "Head too," he whispered. "Or he will."

She rubbed the soap on the rag and scrubbed over the whole of her head, then her torso, arms, legs—fast and hard. A hint of warmth roused her skin.

Rinsed with a final dunk of her head, ridding herself of lingering fleas, she hopped from the tub. The sensation of almost clean felt like a blessing. She rubbed the goose bumps dry.

Before she could cover herself, Rat-Face snatched the towel. "Arms out," he said. "Name?" He picked up a notebook and pen from the bench.

She spread her arms. "Sam Lawson."

"*Full* name."

"Lawson?" said Ned. "You're the one got a letter from...."

"Stop," Rat-Face said. "It's burnt."

Burnt? Her arms drooped.

"No letters. Not in, not out." He tapped the notebook. "Real name. Now."

"Samanthos Lawson."

"And you'll never hear it again." He wrote it next to a number, blurry without her glasses, something-something dash six. "Born?"

"Haverford, Pennsylvania."

"Age?"

"Twenty."

Ned measured her with a tape, and answered the remaining questions. "Arm span: five feet eleven inches. Brown hair, fair skin, high color."

Under the eyes of ogling strangers, who wouldn't have high color?

"Eyes green."

"Six," Rat-Face said. "Step up."

Those prisoners, numbers one through five, who were they? Were their identities gone too? Did they miss them?

Six stood on the scale. The platform wiggled under her bare feet. Ned slid poundage on the bar.

"A hundred-thirty. Height: five feet, eleven." Stringy but muscled. "Feet: ten inches." He jacked an eyebrow. "Bigfoot."

Mamma thought so and made no secret of it, hoping that Sam would shrink. Should they cut off her toes? Bind her feet like the women in Father's Chinese poetry book? It was implied: be more feminine. Something she'd never be. How she wanted to shrink now, here with the full extent of who she was on display.

"Can you write?"

"I'm a professor's daughter."

Rat-Face thumped her head with his pen. "Yes or no."

"Yes."

"Distinguishing marks?"

Ned held a lamp high. "Pock marks, both cheeks. Brown mole, ridge of her right ear." The torn mole had healed rough, thanks to Barth's ring. "My Pappy's crest," he'd gloated soon after the family moved in. Some believed him high born. Maybe even Barth believed it.

The injury Six had inflicted on Barth gave her a snick of satisfaction. Not something she was proud of, though. Her cheeks colored.

She stretched for her clothes on the floor.

"No." Ned handed her a pair of wool pants, shirt, a jacket, weave rougher than a horse blanket.

These pants were baggier than the first pair her brother had handed down. Too many times she'd trodden the hem of her full-length frock, palms skinned, a split lip, rents in skirts. Paul, ten years her senior, her idol, took pity, raiding the attic for clothes saved for their mamma's second son that never arrived. Paul, her idol, her confidant, her fiercest defender against Mamma's insistence, "Girls can't... girls shouldn't... girls mustn't..."— wear britches, ride astride, work at Chesterton's stable alongside Paul. Had she been right after all?

Ned handed her shoes and two pairs of socks next, as well as two handkerchiefs.

24

"Same for men," Rat-Face smirked. "But you're used to that."
He closed his notebook. "Put her away."

Ned tied Six's hands, in front of her this time, and slid the hood back over her head. The rough cloth snagged the mole, giving her a twinge in passing. Fully on, the hood rubbed what was left of her hair, the bristles feeling as crawly as spiders.

He spun her around twice. The spin made her dizzy without the joy of blind-man's-bluff she'd once played with Paul.

CHAPTER 4

THE CELL

I am Sam, that's me
Repeat until I join you

Six shuffled, unsteady in the hood. Wee-Ned urged her on, his soft hand at her back, the direction unknown. Outside, the air came fresh through the cloth, earth stony underfoot, and...

"Stop." Ned's voice, muffled.

Metal wheels on a metal rail sounded through the burlap. Familiar, though rusted more than the door to Chesterton's ten-horse stable, the door Sam had slid open every morning and closed at evening before her return home.

Home: she had to get back, back to the cottage and barn, the animals to feed, land to tend. Had to. She, her family's sole support after Father's supposed accident. He couldn't plow the garden, cut hay for the cow, and Paul couldn't manage either after his bout with the pox.

Her mother, though she thought it improper, would have to work outside the family confines. But who would hire her? An indigent tainted by Sam's crime.

From now on Sam must remain compliant, remain the girl she hadn't suffered herself to be. She had to repent. Be released.

Sam steadied herself, bound hands feeling the door's edge, the wood thick. Thicker than the stable's door. Her fingers touched the metal bar, oddly low for an entrance.

"In." Again, Ned's voice a whisper, as it would be from then on.

At the stable, the bar ran high above her head. This one sat at neck level, short as a cage.

She'd heard of the silence demanded by the founders, but nothing about the size of the cells. A cage? Please God, no.

Her feet stayed planted, arms stiff at the metal bar. Already, compliance strayed beyond her grasp.

He pushed her. No more softness. Her skull grazed the lintel. She tripped sideways, hitting her shoulder against a wall.

Sliding on rough stone, head bowed, she slipped to her knees—a pebble dizzily sinking deep in a vast ocean. She hit bottom. From all sides: a pressure, invisible, all-encompassing.

Sam, swallowed by Jonah's whale. The walls of its stomach close, as if the existing wall at her shoulder encircled her in some fearful digestion.

Even if her hands weren't tied, she'd fear to spread her arms, afraid to know the walls' imminence. Afraid to feel, beneath her fingers, the stomach's slimy surface. On her rump, she held to the stone. Trusted the stone.

"Head up." Without the pull of hair, Ned slid off the hood, the cloth replaced in an instant by a cap of cold. She opened her eyes.

A lantern on the floor jolted entombment into existence, and to her amazement, reality brought relief. The lantern's orange glow ended her Biblical imaginings, the whitewashed walls softened. They reached to a domed ceiling, the height putting a lie to the cage she'd feared. It was nearly palatial.

The space between the walls stretched half-again the spread of her arms, the length of the cell not quite twice as long as both arms extended. The more she accepted the size, the more her notion of palatial shrank.

The floor barely fit a cot, small table, a water bucket beneath. In one corner sat a box of rags, and beside it a heavier bucket-like object sat bolted to the floor. No escape; even a bucket need be restrained.

"You got an in-house privy," said Ned. "Empties itself twice a week." Six had never seen one, though Barth had claimed, "At our estate, my Pappy put in two."

Ned thumped the table. "Bible's here. Make use," he said. "Repentance, that's your job, and no talking, no tapping, no visits except the priest. You can talk to him. He might shorten your sentence."

Priest? Already the Quaker intentions were shredded. Friends didn't have priests. God was their confidant.

Ned pointed to a small cupboard-like door in the end-wall. "You return uneaten food. Complaints of guards go to the warden; complaints of the warden go to the inspector." His voice softened, "But don't complain."

"Be good and you get yard time. If you're very good, you get a job."

He waved his hand at the ceiling where a narrow shaft rose into the black. "'The eye of God,' light to read by tomorrow."

"My glasses." Without them, reading would be a trick, and without God's assistance, the book would be useless.

"No talking," he said. Holding the lantern by its handle, he limped out, leaving Six hunkered against the wall. The door rolled. Her scalp prickled. With a resounding thud, her world went black.

I could hear all; no stone could keep us separate.
Six and myself, strong together.

CHAPTER 5

SILENCE

Silence aquatic
chest to neck to mouth
Fills nostrils Floods ears

Sam knew silence, a balm found on her first visit to Quaker Meeting. At four-years-plus, old enough to attend, this felt like adventure.

She'd awakened, thrilled at the thought of a peopled expanse she'd never seen before. Others would see Sam. About this, she caught a nervousness from Mamma.

"Hurry, sleepyheads," Mamma in the kitchen. "Sam, wear thy frock."

Sam thought their conflict over britches had long since ended, figuring that her abilities on the farm outweighed her parents' mistrust of change.

After much frowning, they'd acquiesced to her calm insistence. Sam in britches and shirt turned out much like the gray-frocked child, respectful by and large, inquisitive, accomplished at the tasks at hand and her studies too. Sam assumed clarity had come.

Minutes later, dressed in her best, Sam, the last to be seated, slid into her place at the table.

"Britches?" Mamma said. "Thee'll be a spectacle." She pointed at Sam's room. "Change."

Sam quietly ate her porridge. Quakers didn't argue. Argument accomplished nothing.

Father finished his meal and took hat, coat, and scarf from the peg by the door. "We have to go."

Mamma's jaw set. "This is a lie. I won't have it."

It always came to the same thing—what was, will be. Girls don't wear britches.

Sam remained insistent. She refused her mother's drab habits. In the spirit of compromise, Sam wore her hair in a braid down her back the way her grandfather had. She too could live the old ways. Yet conflict with Mamma festered. "Thee's so stubborn," she said.

Paul laughed. "We'll call her Sam-mule."

"There's no funning here. What will people say?"

"They'll assume she's a boy, and that's on them." Her family wouldn't outright lie. Lying was not the black and white she'd been led to believe. So hard to detect, this art of careful shading.

Following Father to the door, Paul said, "If God wants them to know, He'll show them."

"How can she find a husband?" questioned Mamma, the heels of her hands at her temples. "Already, thee's too tall, too boyish." She turned to Father, her eyes imploring. "What future?"

"For pity's sake!" Father said. "She's four!"

Without a hug, Mamma helped Sam into her jacket and muffler. "Clarity will come," she said between clenched teeth.

Sam had clarity. The fog belonged to Mamma.

Sunday, it had snowed. The four of them, snug under a blanket, headed for the meetinghouse—Paul, Mamma, and Father shoulder to shoulder in the narrow cart, Paul in the middle, Sam on his lap, Father at the reins. Last night's snow deadened the clop of Jefferson's hooves and whited the forest.

Large and larger flakes slid through the windless morning, the whole world muffled. Gentle creaks from Jefferson's harness only emphasized the quiet.

The expanding world filled Sam with awe, and she greedily absorbed bends in the road leading to wider and wider vistas.

By mile three, a wind picked up and tossed the quiet aside as one would a cloak come spring. But it wasn't spring.

The snow invaded the gaps at their collars. Cold spilled down spiral canals, drumming Sam's ears until they ached.

At the meetinghouse, Father tethered the horse with the others in a three-sided shed, and the family jumped from their cart. Bending into the wind, they trudged through drifts above Sam's knees.

Father opened the wood-paneled door. "Quick now." In they went, stomping snow from their boots. He shouldered the door against a blizzardly howl. The latch clacked, and quiet surrounded them along with warmth and the smell of wood milled before her grandfather's time.

The family stripped off their mufflers and coats as they passed the potbellied stove, the metal taller than Sam. Vents in the belly glowed red as they settled on hard benches. Mamma sat sequestered with the women; Paul, Father, and Sam kept to the other side of the aisle.

Sam listened to the snowmelt drop-dropping as unknown neighbors nodded, and smiling, slid onto the bench.

In silent worship, Sam knew she should be open to God. She'd been told, "God is love." But her mind and eyes wandered the one big room. She counted the heavy beams on the ceiling, the knots in wood paneled walls. No one took notice.

Finally, eyes on her lap in shy expectation, she waited. She envisioned His presence, a giant descending a beanstalk. Big boots. A beard.

He didn't show Himself.

He might slip down the chimney like Saint Nicholas, but the potbelly's pipe rose narrow through the ceiling. God had better be skinny.

Tired of waiting, she examined the people. The women, with their bent heads covered in plain bonnets. She knew they hid long hair like her mother's, plaited, the braids twisted on top of their heads. All in plain gray frocks.

The men wore broad-brimmed hats with more hair showing, long or short, wild or neat, a variety of beards bushing their cheeks. Her father's, neatly trimmed, complemented hair loose to his earlobes. Unlike the women, each man maintained an identity, and God didn't seem to mind.

God better arrive soon. Did He always run late to His own gatherings?

He would come. She wanted to believe.

Nothing black and white
Nothing but shadow artists at work
Nothing but men made in His image

CHAPTER 6

FIRST NIGHT

Dark immediate
The dark monstrous

Six, again in the whale's stomach, kept one hand to the wall. Her heart thumped in her throat, breath quick. If she released the anchoring touch, her compass would spin and confusion would take her.

Safe by the wall, she pictured the cell's layout. Took a deep breath. Took another, slower. Deeper.

Her full bladder asserted itself. She dared stretch flat on the floor, one leg kicking where the in-house should be, and "Ouch." Cast-iron. She hooked the base with her foot, and letting the wall go, curled to the bowl. Her arms twinged.

She stood using just her legs, and sat, rump to the cold rim. Blessed relief, though gratifying, wasn't the promised alone time.

Six needed peace so she could talk to God, assuming He lived in this fortress the way the founders claimed. But she wasn't a child lost in the dark. She knew where she was. Her family knew. Survival: she'd make it hers.

Palms sliding against the wall, she fingered her way to the cot and sat. Location sure, she stretched out on the cloth-covered cornhusks. Dry stalks poked through her shirt, making her miss the whispered comfort of the straw in her mattress at home. She pulled the cover to her chin, and beneath the heavy blanket of darkness, her hitched breath seeped out through her mouth.

Her eyes leaked. The in-house released its fetid breath.

For her attempt on another's life, the judge had passed down fifteen years.

The stretch of years beyond tolerance, she turned home to times before she knew the call of money. How its siren turned some men blind.

She went back to a time before Kane and his son had set their sights, before the accident—as Father insisted on calling it—to a time of trust in the Chesterton way. Time-honored, a hierarchy where everyone knew their place, where he reigned with grace and tolerance. A man untutored in shadowy arts.

Words my friends Favorites roll
from my tongue Ann-thro-po-o-o-morphic
Delicious caramel lips to teeth to tongue Sa-cro-o-sanct
Or Ser-r-r-an-dip-dip-dipitous.
Meanings a mystery No need to unravel
Yet.

CHAPTER 7

READING

Key to the future

Looking like mother and son, Mamma and Sam shoveled stalls and bedded straw while Father taught school. He tutored Paul most evenings.

Father had taught at the university but preferred the one-room schoolhouse, teaching the unschooled. So it had begun, but word of his credits brought a cross section of pupils—not socially, though, leaving him to himself as he preferred.

While Mamma washed supper dishes and set the bread rising, Father and Paul sat at the table and poured through medical books, volumes of Shakespeare, poetry, presidential biographies, books of numbers. Ledgers. The Bible. A feast as important as food.

Sam loved them all, especially the stories, poetry, and pictures of broken bones set to heal. Knowledge, a magical power, hers for the taking so long as Samanthos hid inside Sam.

At five, by day, manure had been hers. She shoveled. She scattered corn, chickens pecking. Evenings, she sat with Father while Paul repeated Keats, Byron, and Blake.

"I know the words," she'd said. "I'm reading."

Father laughed. "Of course you are."

"No really. Listen. 'I was angry with my friend, I told my wrath…' See."

Mamma, hands in the dough. "It's not what you think."

Sam kicked the table leg. She turned the page. Her finger followed slow words, 'And did those feet, in… an—cient times…'"

"Not one I know." Paul checked the page. "You are reading!"

"So, I'll be a professor."

"We'll see," Father laughed. "We'll see."

Keep laughing, I want to say, and gird yourself.

CHAPTER 8

SAM

Still five, stultified before the world of horseflesh opened, Sam's work-worn Percheron lost its perfection. That spring evening a fine-boned dancer, sleek neck arched, deep chest, ears pricked—a mare from Chesterton's heaven—galloped into their yard, Paul astride.

"You're late," Mamma called.

In the stall, Paul had Sam rub down the mare. "A hot-blooded horse," he said, admiring the chiseled head, her wide-set eyes.

At the cottage, Paul hustled Sam to the table. After silence, Mamma asked, "A reason?"

"Jake, what else? He's on a bender." Head of the stable, Jake had hidden in the tack room, swollen fingers wrapped around a jug. The man, intent as an infant at suckle, held the jug to his mouth. "He couldn't walk."

"You carried him?"

"Every day, one way or another." Paul took a forkful of chicken.

"He should be fired."

"Pray he isn't, Mamma," Paul said. "A new man could fire me." Paul's youth at fifteen would count against him.

"I'll help," said Sam.

"Girls can't, not in a stable." Paul wolfed down more stew.

"Why? I'm strong."

Mamma rested a hand on Sam's. "Ridiculous. It's not done."

"I work in our barn." This should have won the day.

It didn't.

And Mamma thinks me redic-dic-diculous
A word her tongue loves

39

CHAPTER 9

THE STABLE

All created equal—these words smooth the road. Too soon stones abound, and she'll know the need of me.

Two months into the summer after Sam turned eight, her incessant pleading bore fruit. Paul returned home before midday. A hold on Georgia's reins, he leaned against the barn door. "Jake's three sheets already. Good time for a visit."

Taller and stronger now, Sam swung the pitchfork, manure thrown into the cart.

"Dump it later," he said, and pulled Sam astride behind the saddle. Mamma stood by the cottage door, hands on hips, lips pressed thin. She shook her head as they cantered down the lane. Clarity, Sam hoped.

Safe under Paul's protection, Sam wrapped her arms tight around his middle. "We're fine, right?" It wasn't Mamma that scared her now.

So close to what she'd wanted, these steps into the outside world. They could be caught, a price levied on them both. Mamma's fog thickened on Sam.

Quaker Meeting had the balm of a loving surround that kept the storms of the outer world at bay, and no one ever looked askance at Sam. Silence was the key. She'd been fine. She'd *be* fine.

Heading towards the stable came with a freshening wind. Exhilaration sewed jitters into her belly. There was no telling who might be watching in Paul's world—the world run by an overlord second only to God—so said the awe in Paul's eye when talking of Chesterton. Sam imagined the man, a long white beard, lightning bolt in hand.

And this *was* a different world. She saw it the second Paul turned into the wide majestic drive toward Meadowvale. Sam could swear, though Quakers didn't, that the mare took daintier steps on the weedless way. No wheel ruts marred the surface like those in their own lane. There was no grassy mound in the middle. No deadfall in the woods.

A smaller drive cut left through woods and along the edge of open fields as around a curve a great white building appeared. Sam shrank tighter to Paul. "The house," she said. "They'll see us."

Paul laughed. "That's the stable."

Sitting straighter, she peered over his shoulder. She'd expected a brown barn. Bigger than hers, yes, but the same board and batten. Perhaps less warped.

Who'd have imagined multiple gables in multiple sizes? A roof made of slate, and sides covered with white clapboard. The only suggestion of animal habitation was a paddock to the left, fenced with posts and rails, and beyond that, the rolling pasture bordered by woods.

Paul put his shoulder to the big door. "Yes, horses here. Carts, carriages, too, and Jake when he can't get home." The door slid. Wheels at the top grated along a metal track. Sam took a step onto the cobbled aisle between stalls. She breathed in the aroma of hay and horse, nothing of cow as it was in Father's barn. Transfixed, she stared.

Around her, well-oiled wood glowed—black walnut walls, the half-wall partitions making square stalls, boards pegged to carved posts and topped by wrought iron bars. The cobbled way ran long, five box stalls on either side, each as big as her family's living room. Sam tilted her head, eyes to the ceiling, mouth open, and took in the intersecting struts attached to dormer rafters.

The mare nickered and with a rustling of straw, nine horses poked their heads over stall doors. Some Sam would come to know intimately.

Under their appraising eyes, Paul unbridled the mare, haltered her, and clipped ropes to tie-rings on the walls, the horse centered. He unbuckled the girth. Saddle over his arm, he said, "Tack room. Follow me."

At the end of the aisle, he unlatched the door without a sound, opened it a crack, and took a one-eyed glimpse inside. He kept a finger to his lips and then tiptoed into a room larger than their cottage. One windowless wall of racks held saddles. Bridles hung on hooks beneath. Floor racks held horse blankets, buckets beside them full of brushes and sponges, and in one corner, Jake sat slumped on a soft armchair. One of his arms hung to the floor where his fingertips curled against a fallen jug. He snored beside a cold woodstove.

At first the scent of saddle soap filled the room, but closer to Jake came the acrid stab of applejack. A fly flew over a desk loaded with papers and circled Jake's head before centering on his nose. His snore turned to a snort. He choked and smacked his lips as if he'd eaten the fly. And liked it.

Paul shooed Sam out and, tack in place, pulled the door closed behind them. "Get the barrow," he said. "I'll scoop, you spread straw."

ℤC℠

Sam snuck in and around the stable at every chance, muscles challenged to greater strength as she grew. She stayed wary of eyes other than Jake's. His, full of rheumy disinterest, caused little concern. She made herself scarce once a week when six-year-old Anna had her riding lesson. Sam hid behind stacked logs split for the tack-room stove and watched.

She could see through chinks in the pile and stared, fascinated, shocked, even. Anna, two years younger than Sam, arrived with a razor-eyed governess. The child was small in a long frock, but oh heavens, the frock—busy with flowers, a garden-full of color, lace at her neck and on the cuffs of her long white bloomers. A different world for sure.

The first time Jake had lifted her onto the saddled pony, he winced and squeezed his right shoulder. Recently, he'd done that a lot.

Anna faced him as if she sat on a backless chair. Tipping, she grabbed what looked like giant rabbit ears jutting from the saddle.

Sam gasped in unison with Anna, remembering her attempt at a sidesaddle ride on Paul's shoulder. She'd been riding astride his neck. He'd pranced around the living room, bouncing Sam to a joyously frightening canter, slaloming armchairs by the fireplace and then ducking through a doorway into the bright bedroom they shared.

"Get thee down," Mamma had said. She theeed and thoued as old Quakers did, as Father did to Mamma. Paul had slipped that habit. Sam never started.

"If thee rides," admonished Mamma from the doorway with not even a thin-lipped smile, "Best be sidesaddle."

"Like a la-dee-da-lady." Paul swung her onto one shoulder. She tipped, legs flailing and clutched an arm around his head as she slid backward and fell to the floor.

Anna's face mirrored Sam's same panic as she wobbled.

"No, no," Jake scolded. "Knee over the pummel." He smacked the upper of the two rabbit ears. "Lift your leg." She clung harder. He shoved her leg, tipping her backward. Her grip lost, she latched onto his collar. He gritted his teeth and pushed her leg over. She swiveled, facing the pony's head, her knee tight to the pummel.

"Right," Jake snapped. "Now calm yourself." He covered her legs with her skirts, tucked the left boot into the saddle's single stirrup, and with slow steps led her around the paddock, her governess watching from the rail.

Small as Anna was, she looked big on the pony, unhappiness clear in the set of her jaw. The short-legged animal trotted. He bounced her unmercifully. A bellyful of cream would've turned to butter, and in no time the governess said, "Enough now."

"So, proper girls do ride," Sam said to Paul later that day as he readied Caesar for exercise. One couldn't get more proper than a Chesterton, though Mamma would certainly frown at Anna's showy dress.

Sam had felt lucky just being at the stable, and didn't want to press for riding too; greed would get her nowhere. But evidence of propriety helped.

Paul mounted the hunter, the pony on lead to finish its exercise, when Sam blocked their way. "Couldn't I ride too? You'd have less work."

"Just because Anna..." He leaned from the horse and wagged her braid. "What makes you think you can ride?"

"I rode Jefferson, remember? You let me." Mamma, absorbed in kneading dough, hadn't noticed.

"Bareback on a workhorse isn't exactly riding."

"You said I'd make a horseman one day. Why not today?"

He glanced at the stable. "When Jake leaves," Paul said. "We'll see."

Having finally dared ask, she couldn't wait. "And not the pony." Now, she was being greedy.

That afternoon, Paul brought Sadie from her stall. Sam couldn't have been happier. Sadie was young and gentle enough to use a snaffle, the jointed bit with a single rein. The curb bit, for hard-mouthed horses, had two reins, leaving the rider with fists full of leather.

Sam felt for those horses, the bit a vicious piece of metal in the shape of a capital H. It had a raised section like a knuckle in the cross bar. Reins attached at the sides, top and bottom. A slight tug on the lower rein would tip the knuckle, gouging the horse's mouth. A hard tug might break the skin. Even worse, sawing would dig a bloody trench in the palate which some riders didn't hesitate to do.

Paul had been right; she had a light touch on the reins and a natural seat. Their practice around the cottage paid off. Beyond that, she shared a gut-level trust with each animal, a mysterious twining she couldn't describe but that grew with loving touch. It was a love returned by the horses. They moved as one in shared understanding, the joy of wind in their faces, crisp winter mornings, languid summer afternoons. They could sense the nearness of animal threats advancing from behind, know the low-lying branches without seeing and duck instantly.

Sam wished this with people, but people had a separateness, a shield she couldn't penetrate. Or did she lack trust, the shield hers?

On one of their outings, Paul let Sam try sidesaddle. He said that sooner or later, one of them would take on Anna's lessons.

Sam hated the saddle as much as the day she'd tipped off Paul's shoulder. This fixed Sam's insistence—it wasn't worth being a girl no matter how Mamma fussed.

And Mamma did fuss. "One day," she repeated often, "you'll be seen." She'd snap her fingers. "They'll fire Paul, your shenanigans to blame. How will you feel then?"

Mamma had a point. How would Sam feel? Sam was closer to Paul than anyone. She'd never want him hurt and yet how could she be other than Sam? He'd been clear—he didn't want that. "Be careful," he'd said. "We both will."

One summer morning, while waiting for Anna's tedious lesson to end, the new governess wandered off and Sam, after watching a while, fell asleep in the sun behind the woodpile. She woke with a start. A high inquisitive voice asked, "Who are *you*?" Anna stood over her with a slight frown, more mystified than disapproving.

Sam, eyes big, fingers to her lips, looked wildly around for the governess and then, one forefinger up, said in voice much deeper than Anna's, "Shhh, please, don't give me away."

"To Miss Priss?" Anna giggled and knelt. An instant conspirator. "Never."

"Annaaaa, where are you?" The annoyed call came from afar on the other side of the woodpile.

"Here." Anna stood and waved from behind the logs. "I'm here."

So much for conspiracy. Three little words—the end of Paul and Sam. A punch in the gut from her instant ally. Woozy on the ground, Sam rested her head against the piled wood.

She'd misjudged. Sam didn't know people, simple as that. Too little person-to-person contact beyond Friends Meeting, and most of that silent. She'd been isolated without knowing or caring.

At the stable she knew enough to stay clear of Jake, sure, the one obvious person. She'd never understand peoples' perceptions. She had no comparisons, no way to learn, and now, too late to matter, she awaited the death knell.

"I found…" Anna's happiness, even excitement, filled every word; her new discovery a thrill. "I found a *dead frog*."

Her words cracked like a whip, the lash thrust in one lethal direction, and with a jerk, snapped in the other direction with a loud, painless crack. The snap cleared Sam's head. She eyed Anna, fingers on both hands crossed behind her. Had the grip of panic been released, Sam would've laughed aloud.

"That's disgusting," Miss Priss called. "Leave it this instant."

And so it started, their secret safe for now. When Miss Priss went for her walks, Anna begged off the lesson early. Jake, only too happy to oblige, left Anna and Sam a few minutes to talk with the horses, investigate the grain bins, visit the kittens in the hay mow. Anything not to ride. "I hate riding," said Anna in Sam's ear.

They watched Paul wash the carriage, or helped brush the pony Anna detested, and then on to the next horse for grooming. Sometimes, they just sat behind the woodpile and laughed. "More fun than riding," said Anna. "I wish I could like horses; Papa'd be so happy."

"We should trade places. My mamma thinks…" Sam was going to say, "girls shouldn't ride." Good grief, a slip of the tongue, all too easy. "…with time, you'll love them."

A sly grin between them, Anna said, "More time like this? I'll ask Papa." She danced a jig. "More *lessons*, that's what I need."

Saturday mornings spread to Tuesday and Thursday after school. "Papa's as pleased as me, maybe more."

Sam reveled in sharing the stable with Anna as Paul had with her. It was a strange sensation, showing Anna the inner workings, Sam playing the owner, Anna the inquisitive child. They snuck around avoiding Jake, more game than necessity, as he spent much of his time in his chair, massaging swollen knuckles.

Paul pretended that he didn't see them skulking about, but Sam caught his indulgent smile as she pumped water into a bucket for the pony or pulled a carrot from her midday meal, offering it on a flat hand to Georgia.

But Sam paid for her bond with Anna, the currency composed of fraught dreams. In them, Mamma's predictions came alive. They festered in the dark. Cast doubt by day. Could friendship be worth the risk?

She hadn't needed friends. So why now? Or was it simply a matter of not having known the emptiness?

Comfort came with shared fears, both of them striving to make their family proud. At least not disappointed, though Sam held her secret close.

It had seemed while working with Paul, her trust in him had been all that she needed, complete until Anna expanded Sam's sense of belonging.

Anna loosened Sam, the way a worm aerates the earth, room made for richer blooms. Together, they could laugh at themselves—something hard to do when alone.

ಬಿ ಲ

Months turned to years and at fourteen, working at the stable had become Sam's accepted position. Sam, slender and taller than Anna, deep of voice as she'd always been, looked far older. But Anna, at twelve, seemed older in the fullness of her robust chest. She moved in fluid steps with a hint of motion shifting her skirts, yet easily climbed to the loft where an instinct to nurture came with every visit to the kittens. She mothered a runt with gentle nudges, moving it closer to a teat the bigger kittens had crowded. And with each passing day she stroked its little body, holding it to her cheek as its eyes opened to a world it would otherwise have been denied.

Sam felt clumsy in Anna's presence, but strong, ready to deflect impatient Jake when he railed against her shortcomings. Sam hated to see him crush her. Anna, so submissive, head bowed, took his word for gospel.

Yet slivers of rebellion snuck in—dead frog indeed—slivers Sam encouraged in hopes of someday taking over her lessons.

ॐ ॐ

All too soon, the eyes Mamma predicted came to pass. Chesterton himself strode down the drive that sunny afternoon, jodhpurs, high black boots, white shirt, a crop under one arm of his tweed hacking jacket. A surprise, since minions usually requested his horse.

Sam stopped mucking the stall. She crouched. Holding the fork close, she backed into a corner. He may have missed her movement, being in the sun as he was.

"Thought I'd take a ride," he said advancing toward Paul who'd been filling a bucket at the trough. "Ask Jake to fetch Caesar."

"I'll do it, sir. Jake's on errand." True: one jug down, he'd gone for another.

"Didn't I see him?" Chesterton waved his crop at the stable door. Sam pressed tighter into the corner. Blame dreams bloomed. Her mouth went dry, her tongue coated in ash.

Mamma's words like so many bats beat behind Sam's eyes. How will you feel, indeed.

"Ah...n..no," Paul stammered. "Sir. Not Jake."

What would he do now? What could he do? Sam peeked through the bars atop the stall.

Her brother scuffed his boot in the dirt. "That's..." he coughed. "Sam. Sir."

"Sam?" Chesterton cast an eye in her direction.

"I'll introduce you." Paul stepped to the stable door. "Sam."

A white-fingered grip on the pitchfork, she came from the shadows and stood tall before Chesterton. She looked him in the eye. Gave a slight bow.

"Another hand?" he said. "I didn't authorize this." The accusation froze her as if she'd hired herself. Which she had.

Her mind awash in the shaming to come, she saw her insistence on boy's clothes coming to an end, the rest of her life suffused in guilt. And worse, Paul's plans for university destroyed. How could she have been so selfish? She'd crawl in a hole. Any hole. But where?

"Sam's in training, sir." Paul turned to her with a quiet command, "Bring Caesar, I'll saddle up." Then to Chesterton, "Training at no pay."

Paul hurried toward the tack room, and Sam ran to the field behind the stable. She returned with the hunter on lead, Chesterton waiting. He tapped the crop against his boot while Paul finished cinching the girth and adjusted the stirrups. "He's all yours, sir."

As Chesterton mounted, he said, "Speaking of pay, tell Jake, when I finish, I want him at the house. Bring the ledgers."

"He may be quite late, sir. But I studied accounting, and I keep the ledgers. I could bring them."

Chesterton frowned. He gathered the reins, and his brow cleared. "That's right, you're Professor Lawson's son, aren't you? So, yes. Have Sam cool Caesar. You and I, we'll look to the books."

80 CB

Now a hair taller than Paul, with long sinewy legs, Sam stood out. Her muscles were defined. Others recognized how she absorbed horse sense. She learned the tone of talk that easily swiveled the equine ear. She assisted at breeding, birthing, and breaking. She learned to spot colic, enflamed tendons; learned how to maintain healthy hooves. No longer a trainee, she made two dollars and seventy-five cents a week to be put toward her studies.

Book learning with Father and Paul fed her every night, but like Paul, she wanted more. University would be far in her future at this rate, but she'd earn more eventually. Paul made twice as much. He'd go in a few years.

She hated the thought of his leaving, no more working side by side. No hurrying through chores maintaining home and hearth, the four of them making the farm run. There'd be no excursions, no more spring mornings spying on fox kits. She'd be on her own, maybe head of stable, so Paul had hinted. She knew her job. A talent for it, Chesterton had said. She could map the coming years with certainty, and it would take years, but eventually...anything was possible. Her future was assured.

Bright horizons cast the deepest shadows

CHAPTER 10

DARK

A world of dark sits eyelids
sits hips pins legs
oh cornhusk misery

A flood of silence filled her ears, rushing as if she lingered by some tidal canal. But no canal is tidal. Then whitewater in the teeth of snowmelt. No, the water would simply rise, flood the locks, invade bordering fields, vex the farmers even more than this flood of argument annoyed Six.

Her chest tightened. The tightness took her away to nights as a child, wary of tentacled creatures lurking under the bed; the grabbing sort that kept her from dangling a foot over the edge. Being four had its drawbacks. As she had then, she tucked her knees, embryonic, under the blanket.

At home she'd loved the quiet, even the night's wee-hour silence after their fire stopped ticking in the grate; Tig, the cat, curled warm at her belly. Safe. She'd forgotten those blessings, along with the jolt of her first enforced silence.

This night's self-argument brought it back, when in kindergarten a new kind of noise found her, along with a stunning new quiet. Silence: the word itself spewed from her teacher's mouth—a noisy word oddly encased in spittle. Yet silence did ensue.

The teacher, no doubt at wits end—dashing here, capping a spilled jar there, intercepting flying pieces of slate-broken chalk—the room a stew of wrestlers in a broth rich with chatter, burble, and clomp.

"Silence," Miss Clancy shrieked, her first attempt through the wail of a hair-pulled boy. Hands on hips, elbows sharp, she leaned at Sam. "Young man…"

Well, yes, Sam had pulled the swaggering boy's hair after he pulled her braid. Her hair was longer than the other boys', brown and so old-fashioned that Swagger called her "Old Man." Wearing glasses like Father didn't help her fit in, nor did being a head taller than her classmates, her voice half an octave lower.

Swagger surrounded her with his pack of chanting companions. Inside the classroom, the taunt stayed meek beneath their breath. In the yard, the pack turned loud, a hoard of predatory chickens pecking at her hair until baldness felt possible.

Hair with red glints. "They're pretty," Mamma once said. "But a sign of temper. Pretty is as pretty does." And Sam, though justified, hadn't been pretty.

Miss Clancy should be impartial. A peacemaking Quaker would be. That silencing day she wasn't, and tired of taking Swagger's abuse, Sam had shouted back. She'd yanked his curls.

Inches from Sam's face, Miss Clancy's upper lip lifted, white teeth bared. It could have been a grin.

No, the ember in the black of her eye shone too fiercely. Then came the second pronouncement.

From behind her teeth, the 'S' of silence hissed. And as if teaching Sam the individual letters, her jaw hinged open for the "I" sound, showing a full set of upper molars.

The pendulum at the back of her throat swung above a white-coated tongue, and the push of her breath in Sam's eyes carried the quavering "iiiiiiiiiiiiii," until the tip of Miss Clancy's tongue levitated behind her front teeth. With a shout, "LENCE" blasted forth, followed by a thunderclap—the flat of her hand smack against Sam's ear. The inside of her head rang, the outer world silent, her ear disconnected.

Sam's lower lip quivered. No one had ever hit her. Quakers didn't.

Miss Clancy *was* Quaker, for Lord's sake. Her covered hair and plain frock said so. Apparently, it paid to look beneath the surface.

Sam, the pretender, had no standing. She didn't look at her own britches. Judge not.

By the next morning at breakfast, Sam's ear remained tender to the touch. "Time for school," Mamma had said, ready to usher her out the porch door.

Sam took her plate to the dishpan and pulled Blake's poems from the shelf. "I'll learn more here."

"What's this about?"

"Miss Clancy doesn't teach letters." Sam touched her ear. "I'll study with Paul."

"What happened?" Mamma took Sam's chin in hand, turning her ear to the window. "Who smacked you?"

"*You* can teach me. You know words. I don't need Miss Clancy." From listening to Paul's lessons, she knew that her favorite poets—Blake, Keats, Byron—had been schooled by their mothers. And Keats, he'd been a stable keeper.

She opened the book. *Jerusalem*—she knew this one—and turned the page. "Where shall we go from here?" The Chinese book fascinated her, not the poems but the illustrations of warriors tall and strong in their armor, and women in strange frocks, their feet tiny as a baby's. The kind of person she refused to be.

"Binding," Mamma had said. "Because Chinese men liked them small and delicate." Not like Sam. Though Mamma didn't say it, Sam heard her thoughts.

"Thee already knows how to read, and I'll not humor thee." She tightened her apron.

"Then Father can when he teaches Paul." Sam opened the bone book and leafed through the pages.

"None of that. No school means work in the house. In the barn."

So began deeper studies at night. Sam didn't miss classmates. Their silly play held no allure. She preferred animals in her barn, their affection, and work fed her sense of value.

Tig kept her company through lessons, warm and companionable. When Tig died, Tig-two purred on. And once, for months when she was fourteen, a rejected foal came her way, teaching her more than any school.

Her Lazarus, saved from the bone pile. She'd kept the colt, cared for him as his legs hardened, knowing already how he would cavort around the paddock. She trained him, her own horse, the stallion of Chesterton's stable, his future as clear as hers at the university.

CHAPTER 11

FIRST DAYS

Six woke cold to the scent of excrement. Not horse. Not cow. Her every sinew vibrated. Her muscles ached, and in her sleep, she'd lost the reason why. She forced her arms to her face. The heels of her hands ground at her eyes.

The excrement, it came to her—human. A nightjar. Surely she'd emptied it before bed. The blanket she held to her nose didn't help. She swung her feet and hit a wall she couldn't place.

At the other edge of the mattress, she eased her legs over. These legs, sheathed in rough pants, couldn't be hers. Surely sleep still held her.

She touched fingers to her chest, the over-large shirt something she'd never wear by night or day. Her bare heels rested on a floor she couldn't account for, and what of these bodily complaints?

At home, it took time to navigate between dreams and the day's solid insistence. She slithered across the disconcerting boarder the way she'd dismount a volatile horse—slowly, right leg over the cantle, left standing in the stirrup, slip the stirrup, bend across the saddle's smooth center, slide belly to chest, smell of leather, slide lower until her toes touch the ground.

But this time, bare feet touched stone. She stood. This, the feel of sleepwalking—not the world of Morpheus and yet not the real world, either.

Eyes closed, she listed sidewise and sat down hard on the cot. She didn't want to remember, yet here sat remembrance fat as a bullfrog compressed between brain and bone.

Eyes open. In the dusk-like dawn the walls and vaulted ceiling, invisible in the night, closed rank. Dim light crept from a shaft rising through a hole in the ceiling to a gray circle not much bigger than a man's head. God's eye, Ned had called it. Was He watching?

Feet on the floor, she set her toes into the seams running between stone blocks. Cold leached into her soles, colder than winter at home. Early mornings there, the wood floor held heat even if the banked fire had died.

Well, this wasn't home. And it wouldn't be. She knew that, and still the mellow oak called. She pined for them—Father would have stern words for a pun as bad as that. This moment of play was a better path than crying.

Why did she feel six years old? Yes, her name was Six, and would be until God knew when, unless Father could persuade a judge to reopen her case. She'd survive until then. She could.

Her need to pass water drove her toward the in-house, a pot she wouldn't be able to pick up much less take outside. An odd sort of luxury, this, considering her excrement would sit—what did Ned say—emptied twice a week.

Strange clacks sounded, and a slot opened in the wall opposite the door. The scent of mush with molasses fought for dominance. It failed.

Nevertheless, after no dinner last night, hunger drove her to the bowl. She took it to the cot, clamped the bowl between her knees, and without ceremony, scooped wooden spoonful after spoonful fast into her mouth.

This offering devoured along with a square of bread, she washed all down with weak coffee. At home her family drank tea in china cups set on saucers with metal spoons to stir the sugar. Sugar—Chesterton's sister would look down her nose at such an adulteration.

Empty dishes returned to the slot, she donned socks and shoes, and from the cot examined the rest of the cell. A Bible— not hers, she had no possessions—rested on a small table against the opposite wall. One stride took her to it.

She leafed through the pages. A psalm or two would help start the day, but the print blurred the way it did when she'd turned four. So distressing, learning to read at three and the words slowly turning too fuzzy to see, until the day she tried on her father's glasses. The print miraculously cleared. She figured this had to be part of Mamma's belief in clarity.

More light might help. She moved directly under the skylight, to no avail. If only she had her glasses.

She'd have to think. Repent without the Bible's assistance. Silence, the vehicle carrying her to God and redemption, as was her stated purpose. Clearly other occupants had used this same book, its leather worn. She riffled dog-eared pages.

The cover closed, she ran her hands over the soft hide and folded it against her chest. "The Lord is my shepherd," flowed through her, a soothing river she didn't need to read.

When Six was Sam, Father insisted she memorize the psalms. "You'll thank me one day," he'd said. Most likely, this wasn't what he had in mind.

Appeal is what he had in mind after the trial, a different judge, one with his eye on the law and not on lining his pocket.

Because I talk with God
because faith is mine
because silence rekindles faith
I believe my will
annealed

CHAPTER 12

CELL

Six paced the stone enclosure, door at one end, food slot at the other. Long, long, short. One short pace and another shorter from table-wall to cot-wall. She ran a palm over the whitewashed surface, fingers reading short gouges. The lines, six uprights with a seventh slashed aslant—these tallied the weeks of a previous inmate. Their weeks, at first evenly spaced, grew crooked. Then jumbled. They faltered, and the lines with their look of Cro-Magnon prayers voiced a message that Six couldn't translate.

Day after day, she read the walls, safe as a kit in its burrow. The dark was a time for sleep she couldn't catch in lock-up, always afraid of the next hour, the next day, the next week, an avalanche of the unexpected, the earth turning to rubble beneath her feet.

Food, such as it was, appeared at dawn and dusk. She calmed in the weekly regularity, one day to the next, and found rest—something home rarely afforded.

In the Quaker-like quiet she could reassemble the shambles left behind after trial, collect the missteps, and construct a plan for putting them right.

Clarity. Yes, Mamma. With quiet reflection, all would come clear.

Wait. Be patient. Release would come.

CHAPTER 13

MONTH AFTER MONTH

Hours strung one-to-one-to-one unsung
but for a spoon in my fist

Six's fingers walked the walls. Fingers talking granite, commiserating when stones told how, chiseled and fit side against side, they'd been mortared to unholy silence. Dear God, make it stop.

She'd failed at patience, and instead clapped her hands. She'd failed at compliance, and instead drummed heels on the floor. Anything to dispel the silence.

And shortly after kicking the wall repeatedly, heavy footsteps scaled the roof. She couldn't see the person, only a hand sliding cloth across the skylight. The eye of God gone blind.

Her legs begged, "Run." Three steps and she bashed the door, ricocheted three stumbles backward, bounced off the opposite wall, right corner, left corner, door-wall, wall of the food-slot. Knocked to the floor, she turned beetle, four-legged, back-stranded, a-twitch in the midday-dark.

Later, lying on the cot, she balled knuckles against her temples, brain softening. Her brain her one tool, her only resource in courting sleep. A chance to dream—thank you, Hamlet.

Ignoring mistaken lines, she crossed hands over her chest and ran through Hamlet's speeches again and again. She recited, without thought. Rote repetition kept the thoughts of death at bay. She wouldn't let the maggot in.

CHAPTER 14

WITH ANNA

Words written in silence
wake me
to where I might go

At the stable, Sam's days unfurled with the joy of muscles tested to full potential. Evenings she spent engaging her mind with floods of words in intricate combinations, stanza by stanza. She committed to memory the skeletal attachment of bones.

She couldn't wait to share details with Anna in their moments linked in increasing connection. So hard to believe Sam could gather this person nearly as close as Tig-two, and just as she settled into this ease, a frantic Anna appeared at the stable.

Not a lesson time. No governess.

"Auntie's sending me away." Tears streaked down her cheeks. "She says I'm thirteen going on thirty, I need 'finishing.' Switzerland!" She wiped her eyes. "Philadelphia would be bad, but across the ocean… it's too much."

Sam would give anything to study in Philadelphia, much less Switzerland. "Finishing? They coat you in oil?"

"Auntie says professors can't teach what I need. Papa wants me home, but he believes her." Anna gave a rueful smile. "Auntie says, 'Learn to be a young lady.'" She bit her knuckle. "She's warned me of men and their hands, the shame of touch in intimate places. She got fidgety about the touch that spoils." Anna laughed. "Once I marry, that touch turns sacred." Her hands dropped to her skirts, fingers twisting the folds. "I guess that could be clearer, but I already know the proper set of a table. I know how to dress. But I'm not to her standard in how I sit, and stand, and walk." She stiffened her back. Leading with her rounded breasts, she walked, head erect. "See, as if balancing a book." Only her legs moved in a smooth glide with a hint of hip. "Soon I'll be as brittle as Auntie."

Being a girl was more complicated than Sam realized. Her stringy body didn't conform, her motions staccato, her stride determined. "I could never do that."

Sam hadn't meant to say it out loud.

With Anna, it wasn't a matter of letting her believe. This lack of confiding went beyond self-protection. It seemed more like treachery. Sam hated the enforced silence.

This secret, too long held in the face of others they shared. Would Anna ever trust Sam again?

Could this slip be born of purpose? Sam's hidden wish?

"You're lucky," said Anna. "You can be who you are. No one fussing at you."

Guilt rose hot. It pinked Sam's cheeks, and she hunched her shoulders. Her late blooming molehills felt like tender Appalachians.

"What's the matter?" Anna reached for Sam's arm as Sam turned away. Anna's elbow bumped her chest. Sam flinched.

Anna stared. Her forehead creased as she tracked Sam's rise of color. Tracked down her body. Anna's mouth opened.

She gulped a great breath and held it for long seconds, lips pursed. "No." She shook her head. "Not possible." Her eyes brimmed. "I thought we were friends." She turned away. "How could you?"

CHAPTER 15

EXPOSED

Nothing but a snail
my shell pierced

"Please," said Sam. "Don't leave."

Anna rounded on her and smacked her arm. Smacked her other arm. "You should have told me." And again, a stinging blow.

"I was afraid."

"Of me?"

"Of missing what's beyond our fence."

"I should tell Papa. Or Auntie—she'd have you drawn and quartered."

It felt like that already. "If they'd asked," Sam hung her head. "I'd have told the truth."

"So you say."

Anna missed her next lesson and the one after that.

Sam waited for termination. Waiting in the midst of Anna's absence made it worse.

Another week and Anna stalked into the stable. She pulled Sam into an empty stall. Sam's lapels in her fists, she shook her. "Don't you ever..."

"Just say it. I'm through."

"You *should* be." Her eyes drilled Sam.

"You mean I'm not?"

"Not yet." She pushed Sam against the wall. "Another secret between us and..."

"Never." Sam nearly cried, and not just from keeping her place. "I promise."

"But why?" Anna shook her head. "Why would you do it?"

"I..." Head bowed, Sam hugged herself. "I don't want to be Mamma. Hobbled and faceless. I couldn't stand it."

"You'd rather be a boy?"

"Not *be* a boy, just learn like Paul." She raised her head, excitement filling her. "I want to read poems and stories. Help animals that can't help themselves. I want to know how bones connect, to splint what's broken." She gripped Anna's shoulders. "And much more. It's all out there. I want it."

Anna poked Sam's breastbone. "So, underneath, you're still a girl." Her eyes filled with tears. "I always wanted a sister." She pulled Sam into a fierce hug.

"No Switzerland now," she mumbled into Sam's neck. "I'll starve myself." She grinned. "Too skinny, and my monthly stops. Auntie won't risk missing a Meadowvale heir."

"And who will you marry?"

"You've ruined the only contender." She laughed. "So, Paul. I've always liked Paul."

"Over your aunt's dead body."

"We'll keep that to ourselves."

CHAPTER 16

JUNE BEETLE

At supper, Sam found herself grinning. She wanted to tell Paul, "Anna has eyes on you." Mamma wouldn't laugh. She'd take it seriously. Too seriously.

Mamma didn't joke about marriage, usually Sam's. Mamma pestered her like a swarm of mosquitoes, "Think of your future." Over and over, as if Sam wasn't already consumed with her future.

"No man will see a bride under those clothes." Mamma couldn't envision a more important life.

That hot-for-June evening, the cottage door open, Sam kept Paul's prospects to herself. A warm breeze flowed through the screen locked against an influx of mosquitoes.

Before the advent of sieve-like doors, Sam hated the pesky suckers, the whine as they circled her head, the neck-slap, slap again slap. The bite. She could use such a screen against Mamma.

What Six wouldn't give to suffer it all again. Mamma. Even mosquitos.

Beyond the screen, a whisper of bigger wings warned that beetles hovered. Their larvae, having feasted on roots and eager for more, had crawled from the dirt. They'd morphed into hard-shell hatchlings, all mandible and hunger, a plague of desires.

They wanted in—at least this one did. One hit the screen, and yet Sam felt the rush of thousands. Insistent, bump-bumping the mesh, the beetle suicidal in its plunge for the light.

Like mosquitos: where one comes she knew a swarm would follow, drawn by the lantern's promise. If they could, they'd feed on the light, more and more of them, until overwhelmed, the flame would suffocate.

In truth, the beetle at their door momentarily stunned itself and fell to the porch, landing on its once protective shell.

Stranded upside-down, useless wings buzzed the floor. Its six legs ran and ran and ran.

Sam couldn't stand the incessant whir and, leaving the table, she pushed the door slowly open so as not to break beetley-wings. She turned the creature right side up and set it free. As soft-hearted as Paul claimed her to be.

"It'll just come back," said Father. "Next time, stomp it."

She couldn't.

But now, Six absorbed the beetle's strategy.

The cell thick in midnight black, she woke with a start. She stretched stiff arms straight up. She waggled her fingers and lifted her legs, feet flailing until almost immediately exhaustion set in.

She couldn't let lethargy stomp her. She wasn't an insect. She kept at it. By day. By night.

Hours of treading air meant slow death for the beetle, but for her, action meant life. On her back, arms wild in circles, she pumped her legs, running, running, all the while careful not to hit the wall.

Flight after flight, the dark made no difference, and a wondrous freedom of mind and body ensued. She soared, anywhere she chose, never bumping a screen much less a wall.

Her muscles took on a new will. She pushed herself. She wasn't dead yet.

> *I swing on memory's thread*
> *breach battlements my body*
> *can't dent*

CHAPTER 17

EXERCISE YARD

The puddle a lake
Ice thick I skate
unlace the blades
and walk home

Exhausted, Six slept, woke to total darkness, and beetling, she soared again. Eat. Soar. Evacuate. Sleep. The rhythm of days without beginning, without end.

Then, sitting on the cot, having felt her way to the food and retrieved another tasteless meal, a sudden light poured down the shaft. What had seemed dim, uncountable eons ago, now flashed brilliant. It showed the bowl in her lap, the grain of the wooden spoon, the latest unidentifiable gray stew. Or was it mush?

The Bible would be easy to read. If she had glasses.

A clash broke the silence. Rust-on-rust scratched her eardrums. The cell door slid. A cold breeze entered, bringing with it Ned's whisper as loud as a shout, "Yard time. Face away, arms spread."

She returned her bowl to the slot and did his bidding. He entered behind her and slid on the hood. The cloth snagged the mole on her ear and then bunched on her shoulders. The snag was merely a minor irritant as she hurried outside.

"Stand still," he said. "When you hear the door close, take off the hood. You have one hour. And Six, not a sound." The outer door clicked shut.

Fresh air. The bliss of it crept through the hood. Two thumbs under the edge, she lifted the cloth and a blast of light doubled her over. Sunblind, eyes buried in the crook of an elbow, she waited for white spots to disappear and pulled the scent of fallen leaves deep into her lungs.

Though her eyes had adjusted, she still couldn't see the trees. They remained distant behind walls three times her height. It didn't matter. Even dead, the scent of leaves brought her the image of spreading branches once covered in fall's bright finery.

And it didn't matter that the yard offered rubble underfoot with a smattering of grass mostly withered brown. She tilted her face to the sky, arms spread.

The leaden quiet had lifted, and beneath, she heard a hint of wind, on it a cricket's song—the creature hidden in a sun-warm crevice. He, a lone survivor this late in the season. His sawing legs slowed with cold, yet he filled the yard, his music ethereal. Would that he might sing forever.

A crow dipped, cut back, and with a feathery purr disappeared beyond the wall. Six wanted it back. With a caw, she'd ask of its mission so close to the city. Could it see Paul at his studies in Philadelphia?

No, he'd be home, at the work Sam should be doing. Six wished she could tie a message to the bird's leg. A carrier-crow. If she had paper. If she had a pen. If she had ink. No letters. Not in, not out.

Would Rat-Face know her voice from the crow's and consider it talk? Why bother? It wouldn't work, and she had a whole hour to take long strides, three at a time before turning. She could see for miles, up between fair-weather clouds into the bluest blue. Giddy with relief, she picked up a rock and tossed it to the clouds, caught it, sharp as it was, and tossed again. A laugh escaped before her hand smacked over her mouth.

Turning beetle had helped weather the dark, but she wouldn't invite a second lid on her cell, or the loss of fresh air. This taste of the yard—it would kill her to lose it.

Strength for release was another consideration, mind and muscle ready for the stable when Father's appeal came through. With no murder attempted, truth will out. Shakespeare wouldn't lie.

They couldn't lock her away forever. That's not the way the world works. She threw the rock. It bounced off the wall and fell at her feet.

She'd have to mark the days as those before her had. With what? And there, the sharp rock waited. She retrieved it, looked around, and tucked it inside her shirt.

Not losing herself in the dark—this was her prayer.

Rock written message etched on stone—
the grating of broken bones

CHAPTER 18

A TOUCH OF KINDNESS

*Ceaseless tears salt wounds
scraped raw
by unimagined grace*

What seemed like seconds later: "Hour's up," said Ned through a small opening in the yard's outer door, the opening covered with a grillwork of bars. Sam kept her back to Ned as she knew she aught, picked up the hood, and pulled it on, careful not to snag her ear.

"Inside," he said, guiding her.

She wanted to say: no, wait. She wanted to tell him about the cricket, ask about the kinds of trees she'd smelled. Don't be foolish. His inquisitive stare in the processing room came back to her. Boyish or mannish, bored or stunned—she couldn't trust him.

She'd rather catch the cricket and keep it in her cell. Maybe tomorrow.

"And Six," he said. "Not a peep." As if he had to remind her.

Inside the cell, her senses in tangled confusion, she tasted remnants of outside air overlaid with fecal aromas and her own unwashed self. The smells flooded her, a layered intensity more than before; the yard had enchanted her nose, touched buds at the back of her tongue, and dissolved the crusted protection she'd built.

With a grinding creak, the door thudded and Six was closed into dense air. Toughen up.

She breathed deeply. More. She hovered over the in-house, teeth grinding. With another deep breath through her nose, she spun on her heel and slammed her fists on the table. Shockwaves ran through her arms—a stupid risk. The Bible bounced. Her glasses clattered beside it.

Oh God—the guards, close enough to hear. She closed her eyes tight, fists at her cheeks, and waited. She didn't want to see the skylight go black.

As she waited, she re-heard the thud of the Bible, the clatter of glasses. Glasses? Her senses had tangled more than she'd suspected.

Could Ned have...? "Not a peep."

At the time, she'd missed the slight lilt of his whisper, the hint of amusement, as if telling a naughty secret. She opened her eyes, almost afraid to look at the table just in case want had run amuck. She checked the door for Rat-Face, the slot for food. Her eyes slid across the wall to the table.

Oh Lord, yes. Glasses. There they were, cocked on the Bible, frame bent, a crack in one lens. Her eyes filled. She picked up the delicate treasure and folded the arms over her ears.

No guard came, only tears.

CHAPTER 19

AT RISK

Early in spring, Sam and Paul stole unguarded minutes together as sunrise glittered over dewy fields. She'd turned fifteen and still loved watching fox kits at play. Taken up with foxy shenanigans, neither she nor Paul noticed how the grass had dried until the kits retreated to their den.

"Jake's gon'a kill me." Paul bolted up from the long grass. He pulled Sam with him, and together they ran for the stable. "Lucifer...." The new stallion on show later that morning—they should've been cleaning the stable, the place meant to be as immaculate as the horse.

"That animal," Jake had claimed, "No one touches but me." He'd announced it the previous month, the day the animal arrived. Lucifer was supposed to be the stable's saving grace.

Expensive as the horse was, he'd been bought to ease the monthly angst—and considerable it was, the bank being uncooperative. With his own stud, Chesterton could save on fees *plus* collect for servicing his neighbors' mares.

Paul had mapped it out, numbers set in columns and tallied for the ledger. The horse, put out to stud, had bolstered income already, though the animal could be as touchy as the flagging economy. A good solid kick where it hurts.

The siblings' run to the stable took too long, even cutting through the woods to the back door. Sam lagged, breathless by the time they turned the corner.

The door stood open. From inside, a clatter of hooves stopped them.

Jake shouted, "You bloody bastard."

Paul crept along the wall to the door. He peered in. Sam, bending low beside him, peeked past his knees. In the middle of the cobbled alley, Lucifer, large and black, fought his saddle.

He threw his head high, breaking one of two straps clipped to his halter.

He lashed one hind leg up to his belly, a vain slap at the saddle that had slipped and now hung low on his barrel, stirrups dangling. Lucifer's iron-shod hooves sparked the cobbles as he danced on a scatter of brushes and currycombs. The stirrups clanged, and in a fright, the horse reared sideways. His eyes rolled white. He wheeled, broke the other tether, and knocked Jake against the wall where he cowered until his knees gave and he slipped to the floor.

Lucifer dashed over him, out and away, the flap of the saddle spurring the stallion onward. Chesterton's "saving grace" sprinted into the distant field, crossed it, and disappeared into the woods.

"You alright, Jake?" Paul knelt at his side.

With the wall's assist, Jake climbed to his feet. He limped toward the tack room. His hand on the latch, he said, "Quit gawping. Find the bastard or we're all out of a job."

CHAPTER 20

REGRET

How could this be
Be me
Be this relentless now

Threats to her work came at Sam from all directions. Jake, a slip of Anna's tongue, Sam's own body betraying her. But the worst of these came from Mamma.

At supper after recovering Lucifer, the story came out—the relief of finding him, the continuing worry that Chesterton would hear of the incident. "Sam," Mamma said, "You shouldn't be there, getting in everyone's way."

Sam stopped eating. "I wasn't in anyone's way."

"She wasn't," said Paul as he helped himself to seconds. "She helped find...."

"I should just end this ridiculousness."

Even Paul stopped eating. "What? Tell Chesterton Sam's a girl?"

"Yes. It's time." Mamma took her plate and, unlike herself, scraped the half-eaten meal into the garbage. "She's a young lady, not that any can tell." She scrubbed the plate in the dishpan.

Father watched from his end of the table. He fidgeted with his napkin as tears filled Sam's eyes.

"Please Mamma, you'd ruin everything." Under the table, Sam squeezed her hands between her knees.

"You won't think of your future, so I have to."

"Please," her voice broke, "if you love me..."

"It's because I love you..."

Sam fled to her room.

And in the cell, here was Six without a job and men taking an interest. Happy now, Mamma?

No, she couldn't blame Mamma. This was Sam's mess. Mamma did love her. Sam knew it then, even if it didn't seem that way. Mamma had been willing to tear up Sam's ticket out; she may as well have been locked up.

Now, truly locked in stone, with no work to turn to, time stopped. If a clock stood in her cell, the weights would hang on their chains, the pendulum still. The wheels silenced.

Gone, the ticking rain of home. She should've listened with greater attention, absorbed the nuance of raindrops on twigs, on branches, on bark, its splat on a dust-covered road. She should've had sympathy for the disgruntled squirrels crawling into hollow trees only to find an owl's haunt.

Elusive sleep plagued her. Night after night, her fingers counted the lines on the wall by her cot: her lines and those of others who came before. The winters, springs, and autumns of their lives and hers overlapped in the endless stretch of nights.

Lost in numbers she couldn't fathom, she started on words. Scrawling blind in small letters, the sharp stone her quill, overlapping letters one to the next in tilted lines visible come daylight, until more ruminations came and overlaid earlier scrawls.

My scrawls looped hers—anger etched in desperation

CHAPTER 21

ANOTHER FULL-ON WINTER

Winds prowl alley and yard
slip on wolfish bellies beneath my door
Ice in the in-house

No sun, and the blessings of the yard came cloaked in a cold flat gray. Six stood centered as the hovering clouds shed their downy centers. At her feet, hard-edged rubble hid beneath the deepening white quilt.

Flakes gathered on the shoulders of her jacket. They seeped into the coarse fabric and dampened her crossed arms. No matter how hard she hugged herself, she couldn't hold heat in her wasted body, and yet the outside graced her with its clean scent as she stomped a path along the walls and warmed enough to let her arms swing to the end of the hour.

Inside, heat, a luxury promised by the founders, had risen lazily from the metal grate in the floor before it faded, forcing her to beetle faster. On her back, legs in the air, and then standing in place, knees marching, arms to the ceiling and back to a silent clap at her sides. Momentarily warmed, she curled under the blanket, shoes and all, tucking scratchy wool close at her neck.

It was foolish to think that heat could travel far in underground pipes. The wood stove at home barely heated three rooms with bedroom doors open to the living room. She knew the cells ran side-to-side down arms like a star. Father's Philadelphia Friends had told them all about the Quaker kindness this place would use to change the world. And yet, she'd gladly exchange the in-house for an outhouse, a wood stove for this supposed central heat. Disgruntled as she may be, she'd never complain. Complaining had a ricochet effect, and she wouldn't risk how it might manifest.

Sometimes, a stray ricochet happened anyway. The coldest morning yet, yes, a tap on the door, and she'd been hooded again.

"It's the furnace for you." Ned whispering, what... Latin? Bastardized Latin at that. If he meant oven, why not say so?

He walked sightless-Six through narrow corridors, her left hand slipping along the whitewashed wall. Down shallow stairs, she fingered the roughening surface. Raw stone. The blocks grew larger the farther they descended.

Easy to trip as he hurried her blind, she hung gladly onto his arm. Odd, the sensation of wanting to feel the give of flesh. From inside the hood a person could be any person—he could be Paul.

"Good behavior." Not Paul, but a kindness in forbidden words. "Warden says your appeal..."

"It's happening?" She seized his arm with both hands. "How...a new judge?"

"Shhh. Paul's letter, he...." He removed her hands just as new ones gripped on the wall side. Someone bigger pressed against her. "We'll take her from here, Wee-One."

"That's all right, I can...."

"I *said, we'll* take her." He pushed Ned aside, and another man hooked her arm. "This one gets special care." She could hear the fellow grin just as Rat-Face had when hearing Kane's directive.

Special care, a furnace? Uneasiness curled her toes. Would they take her to the kitchen, she the prison's fix for a shortage of bread? Pop her in the oven, cook and serve her through the meal slots?

She could use a good warming. This winter her cell had grown colder with every wind-whipped day, wind like critters scuttling, licking, licking at her legs.

If she were a wood frog—if only—she'd stay frozen for the winter and thaw come spring, no worse for the cold bed. But then, she'd be in the woods, mulched under decaying leaves and an overlay of snow, not sitting wrapped in a thin blanket, knees to her chest, shivering on a cot.

And this furnace—if not an oven, then what? Her behavior, yes, she'd been behaving, except for grabbing Ned's sleeve. This system was so skewed; who knew what might be fair recompense for such an act.

Through a door at the end of the corridor, the air turned heavy. A delicious warmth enveloped her. Off came the hood. Before her, in a great room many times the size of her yard, a behemoth squatted. Its hydra of iron arms reached across the ceiling and through the walls. The creature belched as if ingesting a henhouse full of decayed eggs.

"Now for fun," said the bigger, older guard. He grinned at a tall, younger one at her other side. "I'm first."

With a tussle, Tall-Boy locked her arms behind her. Bigger, in front, drew two fingers down the side of her face and caressed her neck. Her head craned away. Tall-Boy wrenched her arms tighter. Bigger unbuttoned her jacket.

"No." She pushed away with her feet. The boy braced backward, "Hurry up," and ground his hardened self against her rump. "I can't wait all day."

Bigger, a hand over her mouth, pressed closer. His other hand groped beneath her shirt, rough fingers, soft skin, hard nipple, and bang, the furnace room door slammed against the wall.

"What the hell's this?" Rat-Face. Should she be relieved or more frightened?

"Just a little fun." Bigger laughed.

Rat-Face shoved Tall-Boy, then smacked Bigger's head. The hand slid off her breast. Both men ran for the door.

The gallop of her heart slowed to a wary trot. Rat-Face pushed her toward the behemoth. "You're a shit-shoveler," he said. He handed her a wide-bladed shovel and tipped his head toward a wall of stalls piled with what looked to be black horse droppings. "Coal," he said. "Now, feed the furnace." He swung open a great door. The creature's mouth gaped, its breath hot.

At the open end of the closest stall, she bent, slid the shovel under loose nuggets at the edge of the pile, and lifted. Heavier than manure. More slippery. The rattling stones fell as she carried her load, and close to the furnace mouth, she heaved her load into the bright center. An explosion of sparks spat in return. She ducked too late, and shrieked, her face spattered, burns stinging, her jacket shot with little holes.

"Keep going, you're not on fire." Kindness only stretched so far.

She kept a greater distance, load after load thrown into the mouth. At first, her muscles jerked with complaint. Beetley flights hadn't prepared her for this, but with speed, the stoking took on a familiar dig and pitch. The coal rumbled onto the blade, and thrown into the red-mouthed furnace, they fretted, the lick of orange flames dancing them red.

The flames intensified. Blue at the base, the coal glowed. Bright pink to white, sparking until another load squelched the dance, only to rekindle again orange. Her efforts created an infusion of heat, an unseen comfort to the faceless in their solitary cells.

For Six, this creation of warmth, not available in Father's cottage nor in Meadowvale, rekindled a small sense of worth. Oh yes, the penitentiary was full of strange luxury, but she should think on her crime, not bask in the fire's mothering pulse.

Her body ran with sweat and she stripped her jacket, leaving it by the door where Rat-Face leaned against the wall. He cocked one foot behind him, dug dirt from filthy fingernails, and gave encouragement.

"If you're hot..." He leered around his bitten thumbnail. "Unbutton your shirt."

Six stifled a retort. Anger at her silence, and the silence that brought her here-and-now, rekindled, and she attacked the coal.

"You know, things could get harder. Much harder." His narrow eye narrowed further. Not the eye of a friend. Moreso the eyes of a witch testing Gretel for fat—testing the readiness to make a meal.

⁎☙

Had I been Hansel, not Willa, I would have told her, Rat-Face didn't test for fat. Skinniness his aim, half-rations all this endless time taking a toll. The end of her menses would leave him free to have his way. Clear to me if not to Six.

CHAPTER 22

POX

Things hadn't been easy at home, either. Paul caught a cold. "Just a spring cold," he'd said. But it kept getting worse—

No one they knew had pox, not out in the country. Pox flourished in the city—all of those people pressed close, breathing pre-breathed air. Father's bone-book didn't cover pox. Sam needed more books.

Wisdom of the day didn't help. Inhale through your mouth, and you won't catch it. It's not *always* deadly—this the wisdom many clung to when sores sprouted inside their cheeks. Be wary!

Of whom? Those obviously afflicted would stay home in bed by the time pustules showed, not wanting any to know that theirs might be the breath that infected a friend, killed a neighbor. "Or," Mamma said before Paul fell sick, "they might be too sick to step past the nightjar." And so it was for Paul. Just a cold, until it wasn't. He was lucky to get to the nightjar, much less to work.

The eastern sky broke gray. Sam had overslept. She threw off her covers and slid back the curtain between her bed and Paul's. He had the window section of their shared room, and, the hour being later than she thought, the sun shone in. His bed next to a table stacked with books should have been the usual rumple, blanket and spread drawn to the pillow retaining the memory of his head.

But no. Breath uneven through his mouth, he stayed prone, only the rucked-up sheet attesting to his unsettled night. That, and the blankets heaped on the floor. She peered close at his face, red as a raspberry, texture to match. The little round drupelets had risen.

His nightshirt stuck wet to his chest, his body hot-hot under her palm. A sizzle wouldn't have surprised her, and when he coughed, she saw the sores on his tongue. He needed a doctor.

"Father," she called. He'd be at school. And the doctor? He could do nothing, what with no cure. But still…

"Mamma." No answer. She'd be in the barn. Sam pulled on a shirt and long pants. Feet into boots. She heard a horse at a clip up the lane, followed by a knock on the door. She saw Chesterton through the door pane, his features gathered in anger—or was it the warped glass twisting his usually kind face?

In Paul's absence, he'd have saddled the horse himself. She opened the door, and his tight mask slackened. "What's the matter?" he asked.

"Paul…" Tears threatened. "The… pox."

Chesterton retreated. "You're sure?"

"His face…," the words, too hard to say.

"I'll get the doctor." Off the porch, mounted, the reins gathered, he said, "You stay out of his room." Too late for that.

Once Mamma returned to the cottage, Sam took off for the stable. Feed and water, and the rest would have to wait.

Chesterton returned before she finished. Despite her push to get home, she unsaddled his Georgia, cooled her, and, as she did, Chesterton said, "It'll take a day or two."

"To die?" She had to leave now.

"No, to get here, Doc has to…"

Two days? What good was that? Two hours, two days— he couldn't do anything anyway. Most likely, he wouldn't risk exposure. Few would. Would she, if the patient wasn't her brother?

She latched the mare in her stall. Sam's feet dragged, boots leaden.

Getting home, being with Paul, that's all that mattered.

"He's hunting a vaccine."

"Huh." Hunting. Doc couldn't come up with a better excuse than hunting some exotic creature.

At the cottage, she took clear soup to the bedroom. Paul wouldn't eat. Getting to the nightjar took his strength, but with little going in, little came out.

The drupelets spread, rashed his trunk, covered his arms and legs, massed hands and feet including the soles, and still no Doc. Sam mopped Paul's brow with a wet cloth. She had to quell the liquid rise in the bumps.

"Never mind," he said as she sat on the edge of his bed. "This outgrown husk…" He rested a hand on his chest. "Be happy for me. I'll be beyond…" He coughed, his body wracked into exhaustion. "…soon."

She could be happy having him out of pain. Not farther. "No, Paul, please, you can't."

"I've no need, Sam. I go to my Father's house, His many mansions…."

"No. Lucifer needs you; you're going to the university. Every person in the county needs you. Please. I need you." She wanted to hold his blistered hand, yet fearful of inflicting more pain, she twisted her knuckles until they cracked instead.

Left alone or not, his circlets kept swelling. They yellowed to pustules and burst by the time Doc came with a liquid more valuable than gold and even harder to obtain.

A-hunting he had been, and successfully. She bowed her head in silent apology. But this vaccine wasn't something a teacher and two stable hands together could afford.

Father and Mamma stood on one side of Paul's bed, Chesterton and the doctor on the other, Sam at the foot. The doctor held a two-pronged needle and a jar of fluid.

"No…" Father began. He passed a palm over his untrimmed beard and turned his mouth into his hand as if to block the words he had to say. "We can't."

"There's nothing to do for Paul," the doctor said. "Keep him comfortable, but the rest of you… the vaccine should keep you safe."

"I'll do this." Chesterton tapped his chest, then waved away Father's protest. "Roll up your sleeves, all of you."

Sam didn't have the strength to think beyond Paul and the glimmer of hope that came when his fever dipped. She clung to this hope as her own body grew hot, the lead of her feet taking her legs. The vaccine had come too late, and soon she too was lost in fever, a giant raspberry stranded on the mattress.

In fever's grip, she saw shadows take down the curtain between her bed and Paul's. Where his had been, an empty space remained, bedding removed, burned as required. A dark bed-sized patch on the bedroom floor spoke of absence, the surrounding wood paled by the sunlight. Absence loud as it echoed from the empty ladder-back chair at dinner.

And Paul. He must be buried out past the foxes. Far from human habitation—a requirement. Was it worse to see the chair empty or to have it gone?

Sam came prepared, or thought she did, as her fever waned. She tried to be ready for the hollow chambers of her heart, for the void in her everyday doings. The air felt too thin to breathe, as if she stood on some distant peak.

Morning, yes, it was morning, a rough hand on her forehead, on her neck.

"It's broken," a deep voice said. Some doctor this was. Sure, she had a stiff neck. Not broken.

"The fever," his voice rose with excitement. "Mamma, it's gone."

Sam opened her eyes. The fever couldn't be gone, what with the doctor beside her, his grizzled image something like Paul. He sat on a chair between their beds, his bed in its place as always, the curtain pushed to the wall.

Knuckles bent, she ground at her eyes, pressed hard on her forehead, afraid the fevered dream would disappear. She peeked between her knuckles. The man didn't have that underwater look, no hazy surround.

Sun shone clearly on him, on the rumpled bedspread of Paul's real bed. Both eyes open, her fingers slid down her cheeks and folded beneath her chin as tears fell onto her pillow. "Paul, it's really you." He leaned in and cupped her hands as he would a fragile bird.

He'd survived; his face, hands, arms, a mass of red divots dug by the pustules. Survived, yes, but not recovered. Exhaustion plagued him. Too weak for heavy labor, he couldn't return to work. Jake must be hard pressed at the stable.

Sam, having received the vaccine, late as it was, had a lighter case. Her divots ran shallow; a minor roughening bearded her cheeks, the rest of her clear. "By God's grace," said Mamma, yet she cried at the sight of those cheeks. "Another impediment to marriage," Mamma had whispered to Father.

But God's grace fell on Paul, or so he said. Being unable to work, it didn't seem like grace at first. "The sensible thing..." he said at supper one night, "is go to university."

Mamma looked as stricken as Sam felt. Even Anna seemed to feel the loss. Philadelphia: the better part of a day's ride away. "You haven't the money."

"I'll stay until my savings run out, maybe get a job."

"In the city?" His plan had been so far in the future, Sam hadn't seen it as anything more than the same dream she harbored for herself. "Now?"

That fall, he packed his clothes and books in a trunk, and, helped by Chesterton's gardener, loaded a horse-cart. Mamma hugged Paul and kissed him. She averted her face, but they all saw the welling. Father shook his hand, and Paul gave Sam a loving punch on the shoulder.

She caught his fist. "I'll miss you," she said, and hugged him.

He'd always been excited about going to the university, yet that day, joy couldn't lift the droop of his scarred face. He squeezed Sam's hands. "It's up to you now. Do us proud," he said, and climbed up onto the bench. With one quick glance at the three of them downcast together, Paul faced forward, down the lane. "Let's go," he said to the driver, who urged the horse on with a flick of the reins.

"Write," Mamma called.

As the cart approached the end of the drive, Anna appeared, surprisingly alone. She waved a dispirited hand to Paul as he passed, then turned back toward home.

"Wait." Sam caught up. They'd trudge the long road to Meadowvale together. Clearly, his absence was a lonely meal Anna and Sam both shared.

On returning to the cottage, Sam pushed aside the bedroom curtain. Paul had left the bed crisply made, no wrinkles in the spread, no dent in the pillow. Better than a bare section of floor, but not by much.

The empty ladder-back stayed at the table, promising his return. A year? Two? An eternity.

After Paul left, she took on every aspect of the stable work including the orders for feed and overseeing hay stored in the loft. Jake returned to his old comforts. He had no reason to bring back others, especially with the stock down five: no brood mares including Georgia, down one carriage horse, Miss Chesterton's gelding—all sold. Anyway, the woman never rode.

The houseboy who brought orders to the stable had disappeared, and Cook's seven-year-old son took his place, at least running the errands, and the four gardeners had been cut to two. Anna had pled for no governess, and necessity made it so.

Sam kept to the master's immaculate standards and beyond the stable, in the main house, under the eye of Miss Chesterton, she set the table for occasional formal dinners, laid out the proper silver, and served spirits as the guests arrived, working into the notice of Chesterton himself. He claimed that he had an eye for integrity and proved it by entrusting Sam with his much-doted-on daughter, the fifteen-year-old Anna. She hadn't told him how well she already knew Sam or how much she missed Paul. And in the aftermath, Mamma's threats of secrets spilled in Chesterton's ear all subsided to grumbles. She saved them for the nightly dough she pummeled and prodded.

CHAPTER 23

STAR-NOSED MOLE

*A careless tongue makes crime
of whispered psalms*

Rat-Face, with a cocked ear, seemed ever-present since he revoked Six's furnace reward. Daylight gone dark and dark and dark.

The newest came for the sake of recited poems. Had they spilled beyond her tongue's silent touch of teeth? Surely not, yet again the eye of God blinked shut, and in constant night, she made herself a star-nosed mole—every sense turned to touch.

Pale hands large at the end of her ever-skinnier arms, talon-tipped fingers, her nails unclipped, and missing only the mole's furry tail, she tunneled from cot to in-house to food slot.

For spilling, she must content herself with seeing the walls with those myriad pink fingers. The tentacle touch, intimate with stone undulations, measured corner to corner and back. She read them like lines of script, more than a book's worth, a whole library of lines taking her to places she'd never have known if left to her previous life of noise, manure, and muck. Or so Six told herself as she floated blind in the silence.

Taking herself to the past, she made her own light where she stretched on the grass of the upper pasture, watched two vultures circle the clear sky. So doing, Six whispered her way through endlessness, rekindling old fires, that she might reweave the unraveling that made her this star-nosed mole.

CHAPTER 24

LETTER

Hope
that winged dove

Reprieved and in the yard, Six circled left, wall-to-wall and took great gulps of chill air, her eyes cast to heaven. Cirrus wisps cut the blue, bringing a flutter of wings she'd all but lost. Her face to winter's thin sun, she basked in its insistence—spring cometh.

A scratching at the outer door stilled the dovish wings. "Well, well," Rat-Face huffed through the bars of the door's metal grate. "Being a good girl, are we? Out of blackout. *And* yard time! Lucky you."

He tapped the edge of two envelopes on the bars—envelopes torn with inquisitive fingers. "*And* a letter? One for me. And could it be, one for you?" A barely suppressed excitement hovered in his voice, but the thought of a letter blotted the rule she knew perfectly well.

She ran for the door. "A lette…?" Oh God, she'd said it. But a letter…

Father? Her case appealed?

Mamma? She didn't know what to hope for, but oh, the beating in her chest.

A letter to her. She, a person after all. Not buried. Not dead. Not forgotten. She threaded her fingers through the metal crosshatch.

"Oh dear." Rat-Face tapped his lower lip with the corner of one envelope, her real name on it. Paul's writing.

"…I could tell you," The Rat said, "but no. It's too sad, and at such a happy time. It would only upset you."

"Oh please, you've got…"

"Oops! Was that you, Six?" His left eyebrow cocked. "Talking? And the other rule?" He rolled his eyes upward, as if thinking hard. "About letters?" Eyeing the address, he tipped his head. "I guess it's not for you anyway. It doesn't say Six." He turned over the envelope and slid out the letter.

Six tightened her fingers. They went white on the dark metal. She'd shake down the door if only she could, throttle him and snatch the letter.

"Should I read it anyway? Mmmm, 'Dearest Sam...' See, not for you. 'I wish I didn't have to tell...' Oh too bad, I guess whoever this Sam is will never know what ..." He turned the letter over. "...what this Paul wanted not to tell." He crumpled the paper and shoved it in his pocket. "And this one..." He waved the other envelope.

"This one's for your next warden." He gave her a conspiratorial wink as if letting her in on a secret. "And that would be..." he paused, "me! There's a mansion in my future. And you." His smirk turned hard. "You're mine. Any minute now." With the envelope, he stroked her bloodless fingers.

"Hey," came a shout down the alley. Another second and Ned pushed Rat-Face from the door. "Warden wants you. Pisser mood, better hurry." He leaned back, looking after Rat-Face as he hustled. Then back to Six. "Somethin's up, can't be good." And he too was gone.

No feeling was left in her fingers. All of the blood had leeched from her hands to her brain, where it boiled.

Having done as I should not
Words of complaint I fear will fly
Pigeon homing
on its tongue
a taste for flesh

CHAPTER 25

SIX

OF FLESH AND SOUL

*How is it I find myself inside
this one random head
and no other*

Within these walls, though she be a human with a will, these men chained her to their petty desires. Even outside, women in wide skirts stood in silent obedience. Obedience, she would not tolerate.

And so she remained deeper than death, where it would take more than the earth's quake to break her free. It would take the hand of God, should He find her here, invisible as she was. Invisible even to Him. Assuming He exists. Assuming she believes.

Cell-bound, she looked to a world beyond Stygian waters and listened to her heart tick. Ticking minutes, clocking hours, massing a fortnight of nights, a moon's-worth of God's blacked-eye. She, buried alone, not so much as the company of bottom dwelling trilobites—alone below the crust of animal breakdown, of plants; below granite, gravel, and sand. Below silt. Below mud. Six, the lowest squirm of existence.

CHAPTER 26

ALONE

Ever seeking
repentance I can't find

Six woke to a dark deeper than behind her eyelids. How many days had dragged their knuckles on the ground?

She reached towards where she could feel the slot. No glimpse of a hand there said that a person stood on the opposite side. No flicker of candlelight crept through. Only the rise and fall of silence.

Once a believer I
now skeptic
stranger to myself

CHAPTER 27

BARKING AT ANNA

The personal touch, the one-on-one, didn't work with Jake standing in the middle of the paddock. Anna, sidesaddle, in frock, warm jacket, and gloves, rode circles around him. He licked his lips, his prodigious Saturday morning thirst all too evident. He liked to say, "Tis the March chill makes me shake."

"Back straight," he barked. Sam could see the effort it took to tamp the volume between his teeth. "Straighter."

Showing below her skirts, the heel of her black boot rose as her head lifted higher on a ramrod spine, the natural rhythm with Caesar's canter lost.

"No, no, no, heel down, elbows in." Jake squeezed his temples between thumb and forefinger. "Rein looser."

Switching the lead hoof, Caesar shook his head. The curb chain jangled. Anna's whole body tightened.

"Oh, for God sake, do it right or you'll never jump." Jake climbed the paddock fence and hobbled toward the door where Sam had been watching. "Get out there," he said and, leaning over, gripped his knees. "Make her practice."

Anna reined Caesar to the gate, her eyes red. She turned away and swiped her cheek with a sleeve. "I can't... do this," she said, then faced Sam. "If I can't jump, I can't hunt this fall, and Papa won't be happy."

"You have all spring and summer." Sam rested a reassuring hand on her knee. "It's not you. Jake hurts. Pay no attention." This was said low enough for only Anna's ears. "Besides, you had the touch to begin with."

She sniffed back her tears. "You think so?"

"I know so."

The next week, Chesterton charged Sam with fostering Anna's attachment to Caesar, while training both daughter and horse for the hunt. Anna, his only child, inheritor of the estate, needed firsthand experience. She'd be a manager until the day she was married.

The future of Meadowvale guaranteed her Papa's attention. She used his own words to persuade him—more time imperative at the stable—and he acquiesced. "If only I could manage Auntie as easily."

Planning a wedding, no matter how distant, had Auntie salivating. Anna told of Auntie delving into a carved armoire full of day clothes, evening gowns, delicate pumps, negligées, robes. And two "glory chests" already full, lo these many years. Linens she'd embroidered. "*Her* marriage bed in mind," Anna had whispered with a suggestive glance. And most importantly, a white gown yellowed with age, the train crisp to the point of breakage.

Auntie's hopes had been dashed, and no one had dared deny her the grieving. Might as well call her a widow, when "My Herman" succumbed to yellow fever. Those once determined hopes she now attached to Anna.

Switzerland put off for another year, Chesterton had already assigned Sam to see Anna safely to school and back as well as to late afternoon lessons, and though glad she was of both, it was a lot of work on top of mucking and grooming. At least Jake, swollen joints or not, cleaned and oiled the tack.

Like so many mornings, Sam rode up the drive one glorious late spring day. Tips of green had breached the winter-brown crust, verges scattered with promising shoots that had swelled. And swelling more, unfolded to a profusion of white and yellow flowers. Someone having let a crocus loose; it multiplied in pricks of blue across undulating lawns all the way to Chesterton House.

Sam loved to dip her nose in the first crocus, then the daffodils and tulips, taking time she didn't have. She went on foot, leading two horses up the lane to collect Anna. Out of reach, the dogwood blossoms tantalized. Small trees having matured, the easterly breeze shared their nectar.

Entering the circle in front of the old stone house, Sam swung back in the saddle, Caesar on lead. She caught sight of Anna, auburn hair in braids over her shoulders, perched small and vulnerable on the granite steps. She sat between the smooth pillars of the porch, her arms around her frock-covered knees. Anna, looking younger than her seventeen years, triggered Sam's protective instincts.

Anna dangled two books bound with a leather strap wrapped around her fingers. She reached for the top of the two-pronged pommel, a hand to the cantle, and tucking her boot in the stirrup, mounted Caesar. Sam admired the casual sling of her skirts as she settled her leg around the pummel, books in her lap. She made it look easy.

"The woods trail today?" Anna asked. As Sam suspected, Anna's dislike of anything horse had vanished once Jake ceased oversight of the project.

Sam could see in her eyes the thrill she found in launching over tree trunks across the path. Earlier in training, Sam had stressed timing the approach, but Anna seemed to have it without thought, learning the way Sam had when she'd been small.

What a pleasure to watch Anna's natural shift of weight, horse and rider one as they leapt, airborne, the float of a thousand pounds of horseflesh, she and the animal united in silent passage. And then down, the earthbound thud and thunder-on, trees flashing dark-light-dark. Opening into adjacent fields all too soon, they slowed to the schoolhouse.

Talk-talk without saying a word—Anna could communicate as warmly as a cat purring. Sam's new sister opened a world of friendship she hadn't missed, and now never wanted to be without. Anna waved from the schoolhouse door, and Sam walked the horses home, their lather long cooled by the time she reached the stable.

After school, she and Anna returned riding abreast. An easier pace allowed for words. "So, what did you learn today?" Sam leaned in for her answer.

"You wouldn't believe the other girls," she said, "all a-twitter. It's that…" her voice deepened, "Bartholomew Kane." Then, back to herself, "A new boy, expelled from boarding school. He's a rooster, always strutting." She laughed, but a frown creased her forehead. "The others simper at him, so why bother me?" A horsefly buzzed around her head. She smacked at it. "He grabs my books, says, 'let me,' and sulks if I don't." They rode a bit in silence. "Mostly, I talk with your father. You're thoughtful like he is."

"It's the glasses." Sam peered over the rims.

"But no schooling," Anna's head cocked the question. "He told me."

"Schoolhouse learning isn't the only way and I want more—university like Paul, to know the happenings now, and of history. I want to read a million books." Catching her excitement, the horse sped up. "Saving enough, that's the problem."

Odd how easy it was to tell Anna these dreams. Maybe riding side-by-side watching the trail made it possible, or the openness of her attention.

Anna kept pace. "You'd go to the city?"

"I'm torn." Sam was, and only now realized it. Unlike the schoolhouse, the university held the secrets she wanted unlocked, and that meant leaving the peace of the woods and the fields, trading the communion of horses to dig in the minds of men and maybe women, at least for a time. She could always come back.

"Do you think Paul's torn?"

Sam wondered if a spot hollowed inside him, too. Empty as his ladder-back chair. Could Sam stand to be away like that?

Or did Paul have the very thing she wanted: to know, to understand, to be a part of congregant wisdom made whole by the weave of dissimilar minds?

Paul's few letters mentioned herds of young men immersed in lectures, later discussed in small groups at breakfast, dinner, and supper; pondered while brushing teeth and dressing, an intensity unleavened with the quiet of home. And yet there seemed to be a loneliness. She didn't have to see blue circles beneath his eyes to know the weight he hid from their parents.

Mamma was sad enough at his absence. She missed the young man she could be proud of, the offspring she didn't have to hide.

Neither Mamma nor Paul would admit to loneliness. Neither wanted to inflict more hurt on the other.

If Anna went to Switzerland, Sam would be bereft. "Anna," she said. "Would you be lonely, if you left Meadowvale?"

"Auntie whines, but Papa says that school with your father is enough. Jake, Papa, and you will suffice for estate matters. Until I marry. But I don't like Jake, and I'm not sure I want to marry. Auntie says it's my duty to Meadowvale." A sad smile tipped one corner of her mouth. "When she isn't around, Papa says, 'You don't want to end up like...' and then he stops himself."

"It's hard to believe she's your father's sister. Has she always lived with you?"

"Since Mummy died. Papa says I'm a lot like her, even though Auntie raised me. 'More than a sip of vinegar,' Auntie says. Not sure if she means me or Mummy, but if I'm a sip, Auntie's a gallon." Anna put a finger to her lips and made a locking motion. "Surely, such words never passed my lips."

At home in the cottage after supper, Sam studied with Father. She could tell he humored her dreams, yet liked the discussion of books, of word origins, and spilling the contents of his mind to an eager listener.

He missed Paul. To hear Father tell it, many students drifted in class, yet the few eager ones made his efforts worthwhile. And Sam, more eager than most, gleaned every scrap. With that, plus squirrelled-away-savings, she'd be ready when her time came.

Salary discussions with Chesterton made her possibilities even more real. "University." He'd clapped Sam on the back. "If you like, I'll write my alma mater."

If Sam liked? Her head swam with the glittering scope. She could be so many things: a teacher like Father, a professor, a writer. She loved Defoe's *Robinson Crusoe*, hated missing an installment of Dickens' stories. And Fielding. She could be a doctor, able to fix mysterious ills, set little bones and big ones, save a life which otherwise would be lost.

She wanted to go forth, not to multiply, but to learn. To accomplish. So much to choose from, the feast more delicious than Chesterton's most lavish entertainments. If only she didn't have to go to the city.

But here, women were a possession. It couldn't be clearer, from Miss Chesterton sedate in her chair, to Mrs. Kane walking a step behind her husband, to the laborer's wife with a black eye.

Anna, too. At the hunt, she rode in the backfield under Sam's protection, not forward with her father and the other pink-coated men. One day, maybe, if any woman could ride forward, it would be Anna.

No fence scared her. She'd gallop Caesar right at the highest, no whip, no crop, just a nudge of her heel and over they'd fly; she with a straight back, heel down. "Perfect form," Chesterton had told Sam when they all rode home after one of the hunts. "You've taught her well."

Sam wouldn't be shackled to the house, though expanding the family farm enticed her too; breeding her own horses, training them. Her Lazarus, having been spared, could make the stable happen. And with Chesterton's letter, she could do both.

CHAPTER 28

EARLY MORNING GIFT

Blessings of the yard fresh in her nose, Six heard paper fluttering at the alley door. A letter? Six had been tricked before. But this was Ned, his whisper through the grate.

She turned winged bird.

Ned, his smirked delight smeared ear to ear, waved the paper filched ahead of their mutual foe. Rat-Face out-foxed. Ned had slipped the envelope from the pouch, and kept it shy of other eyes.

A new judge to hear her case? Bless Father.

Ned slipped it through the barred window. Paper she could hold. Paul's beloved script, My Dearest Sam…. The shushing of other feet sounded down the alley.

"Give it back, he's coming." Ned snatched, but the paper caught on the bars. Crumpled, it fluttered at her feet. The letter hers, all hers. Noisy the heart that bangs in its cage.

"Quick, hide it."

CHAPTER 29

WILLA

I'd have told her to eat the letter, had I been there. Instead, she slipped it between psalms and closed the Bible, only to open it every day to read and reread of the civil unrest postponing her appeal.

Paul's script wound her in the warmth and scent of home, her father's soothing voice as he read aloud, Mamma's hugs, Paul's belief in achievements she could meet.

Had she focused on the smudged numbers heading the letter, she'd have known the passage of years, not just the hour to hour-on-hour slog of uncountable days, their tally lost in overlapped hatchings scratched on the wall. So many years, and her family hadn't given up.

Those years Kane, under abolitionist siege linked to Father, crushed every attempt to enlist a lawyer. Hen's teeth seemed more readily found than a judge without bias.

Upsetting as the news was, she couldn't stop reading. She smelled the paper. She followed the script loops with her finger as she reread, then folded the creases and tucked her letter safely into the Bible.

And it tore her heart the day the priest came offering the word of God, claiming he alone could translate. Certain that Six in all her manifest ignorance wouldn't be able do it herself. His noise attacked the power she found in silent communion, and stripped her—as if he meant to—stripped her of the good side of silence.

Found the forbidden and used it.

CHAPTER 30

FIRED

Another good silence. Nothing had been said about Lucifer's escape with the saddle slipped under his belly, but Jake had warned them. "Find the bastard or we're all out of a job."

She'd put it out of her mind until Cook's son came running one late afternoon. "Master wants the saddle." He stopped at the stable door, puffing, hands on his knees. "Says Jake knows the one."

All this time, that terrible day had come to naught. Sam figured God smiled. But, with the word *saddle*, the chase resurrected. Back then someone must have seen rider-less Lucifer streaking field to woods, saddle flapping below his barrel.

Seen with an outsider's eye, it could seem funny, until later, this incompetence revealed to Chesterton, the incident waiting to be used. Something saved to denigrate the eminent Chesterton.

That long past day, she and Paul had set out after Lucifer, no time wasted, bridles only on Laz and Caesar. Bareback, they'd galloped across the front field and into the woods following rucked-up turf. The divots showed circles of panic. Torn bark scarred a trail through the trees, and at the base of one, they found the demolished saddle, girth mercifully torn, one stirrup missing.

The irons, they had to have whacked his ribs, belly, elbows, knees. God help them, not his sheath. Not his scrotum.

Tight-lipped and intent, Paul had led the way. Sam, hampered by tears and the fear of Lucifer's wounds, left the tracking to Paul while her eyes roamed the distance.

Breaking from the woods, she spotted the stallion where he'd cut back on a distant hill, heading for a neighbor's cornfield. "There," she shouted at Paul.

"Drat." If they chased him through the corn, they'd do damage and word would get out.

"Head him off." Rein hard on Caesar's neck, Paul angled across the field, a shortcut that would block Lucifer's path. Sam followed and, closing in on Lucifer, they saw up-close his white, lathered sweat. To their horror, red streaks ran across his belly. Paul urged Caesar onward, until they were neck and neck. Just short of the corn, Paul caught the broken rope swinging from Lucifer's halter.

Caesar crowded him into a turn toward home and Paul had slowed both horses, coming to a stop before passing the rope to Sam. She held on, crooning softly, while Paul ran his fingers through the lather and over every inch of the fidgeting horse.

"Nothing deep," he said. "I'll get him home, clean him up— you get the saddle."

Back at the stable, they found the only damage to Lucifer was a missing chestnut, the scabby-looking thing on his left front leg, most likely torn off by a stirrup.

Paul cleaned the wound, staunched the blood, and dried him. He checked the sheath and washed the contents, knowing that prospective breeders would probe there first.

She'd worried about the swelling of unseen bruises, but by then the review of Lucifer's prowess had been complete, and in the end, Lucifer proved himself, making all parties happy. Until now.

With the incident come to light, trouble ensued. On Jake's return from his meeting at the house, the red of his bulbous nose had spread down his jowls. He glowered at Sam. "Stupid kid, a botch job on the God-damn saddle, and *I* get fired." He shook his fist. "From the start, you shouldn'a been here." He kicked a bucket out of his path. "Now it's your turn on the block." He laughed, harsh and mirthless. "You'll get yours."

Sam walked to the house. Butterflies, a kaleidoscope in her chest, fought to see if swallowtails could fit up her throat.

She brushed her loose pants free of hayseed, tightened her suspenders, scraped her grimy soles on turf by the side of the lane, and rubbed her boots against the back of her pant legs.

None of it made her more presentable at afternoon tea in the Chesterton living room.

The man himself sat in a carved armchair, relaxed with one leg cocked on the other knee. He wore an open-necked shirt, hacking jacket, dark, knife-creased pants. A teacup and saucer sat on a table at his side, tea cooling.

Miss Chesterton, pinch-mouthed, sat with her spine straight above billowing skirts. She presided in front of a gate-leg table spread with an eyeful of silver: teapot, hot water jug, spirit kettle; each piece caressed until it glowed.

Anna could never become her aunt. She could never speak through tight lips, or pluck at the strings of her neck the way Miss Chesterton did.

The woman poured herself a cup of tea with the assistance of an ornate silver strainer. Tea with no adulterations—she'd removed the sugar bowl and creamer from the tray. Pure she was and warm as the driven snow, sitting with her delicate cup poised, a bird-sharp eye taking in Sam who stood at attention, hands behind her back. Sam flushed.

Chesterton straightened in his chair. He leaned forward, elbows on the carved arms, fingertips pressed together. "An unfortunate incident," he said, without preamble. "No real harm in the end, but Jake's rendition didn't jibe with my informant. Nor did soft hands and spotless clothes speak to his work..." Chesterton seemed about to say more, then spread his hands in silence.

Behind her back, Sam ran a thumb over her calluses. Her flush cooled.

"Young man, I trust I can count on you." Chesterton had always taken her as she was, never suggesting he knew or didn't know irrelevant personal details. Miss Chesterton wasn't as amiable.

The interview over, Sam barely out of the room, she heard the woman say, "Ryan, something's amiss with that boy. The way he looks at Anna. You're too trusting."

"Now Martha…" Sam didn't hear the rest, but she knew the kindness of his soft face, the easy way he sat in his chair and even the way he rolled his sleeves in summer.

Looking at her, Chesterton had always seen a boy—no doubt that was his expectation. He trusted his eyes as did everyone else, even his suspicious sister.

Despite what Jake may have claimed, Sam wasn't fired. In fact, Chesterton made her head of stable, not something he'd do if he had the slightest inkling of Sam's deception.

She grinned and wished Paul could witness this day, hers already more than a woman's lot. She wrote a letter that night, assuring him he'd be headman once he returned fully recovered.

The weeks unfolded with satisfying smoothness despite the hours being full to running over. She started well before dawn with morning feeding and mucking. Then, in time for shepherding Anna to school, she changed to high boots, jodhpurs, a white shirt, and tweed jacket, provided by Chesterton, making her look much like the man's son might have. If he had a son. Sam represented Meadowvale. A big responsibility; it weighed on her, made her wakeful.

CHAPTER 31

UNDER THE MOON

Below God's eye
I lie this sweat damp bed
and weightless rise
to kiss a toenail-moon

At home on sweltering summer nights like this, Sam, sleepless and sweating, would quit her bed and take to the straw she'd left mounded in the pasture. The wee-hour breeze cooled her and, eyes to the sky, she'd track the moon and its arc across the night. Hard to tell which fed her soul more, the full glow or the sliver's hint at future glory. And when the moon stayed dark, she floated in an ocean of stars until sleep took her.

On spring nights before it got truly hot, she wandered the woods anticipating midnight, when the Luna moths came out, much like a flurry of miniature moons when they mated. She couldn't miss the light green beauties, twisted tails waving in a dance of pheromonal attractions collected by the male's feathery antennae. White body finding another's white body. First on the scene took the prize in the hours of phosphorescent celebration.

Nights before she knew of the Kanes, her wanderings brought her by the Biddle place, gone to ruin since old Biddle died. The once grand house had been vacant except for an influx of feral cats, rats, and clamorous crickets in the living room. The crickets had chewed a last meal from threadbare Orientals. Shakes on the roof had rotted, and leaks expanded multiple portholes welcoming in birds, delighted with the escape from winter's reality.

Luckier birds, called by the sky, winged back through ragged holes while the more inquisitive found themselves deep in empty rooms, and lost, they bashed at the windows, careened against soggy walls, scratched plaster down to lath.

Excretions of panic littered floors and baseboards along with a cluster of black dotted ladybugs, their hollow shells still vibrant red. In the kitchen, below a dust-covered window, the remains of a dove moldered, its body a pile of bone and bent feathers.

Outside, weeds blew in waves up to the windows of the fieldstone house. Its mortar crumbled, pulled free by creeping tendrils.

Though exposed to the elements, the beams of the old house remained true. The ridgepole had stayed straight.

Someone with knowledge and a feel for tradition could bring the place back to its former elegance, clear burdock, root out an army of thistle, of milkweed and purslane that spread progeny to adjoining lands, clogging hay fields already invaded by saplings. That was the hope whispered at the hunt club breakfasts. That hope was the subject of champagne toasts at the Hunt Ball, after Kane, accompanied by his wife and son, had outbid the scant competition.

Gladdening old hearts, he promised rejuvenation. He vowed resurrection.

Chesterton and his sister welcomed the couple into their home for formal dinners, Kane's wife and son to tea. Their welcome, that first fall after construction, included an invitation to join the Hunt, a mounted gathering harder to enter than herding camels through a needle's eye.

Six wanted to stay in the good days with Anna, but Barth... Well, yes, she must admit, there *had* been promising days with Barth.

Sam spotted him on a late spring evening with no idea who he was, just a young man swinging a lantern, out for a midnight stroll in the woods. It didn't seem odd once she found out what he was up to. Certainly, no odder than she'd been, sitting on the ground leaning against a walnut trunk. The walnut's leaves were a favorite haunt of the Luna laying eggs.

She'd been enjoying the peepers, when their music suddenly stopped. A fox approaching? A mink? Nice name for a weasel.

Instead came a stocky shadow, swinging a lantern in her face when she stood.

"Looking for an honest man?" Sam laughed.

"You saw him?" He spun around holding the lantern higher. That's when she noticed a pistol tucked at his waist. "Where'd he go?"

"Just a joke, it's no one." Not a friend of Diogenes, she guessed. Few were, and those mostly friends of Father's in Philadelphia. They didn't wait for moths lilting through the woods.

This fellow, she guessed, must be the new neighbor. A Kane.

"I'm hunting a Luna," he said, and shifted the pistol from sight.

"You shoot them?" she asked, as if to make light of deadly intent. She hated guns. Her father wouldn't have one in the house. He didn't care if the groundhogs took free rein in the garden.

The young man held up a lidded jar. Inside, he'd crammed a pale green beauty with wings wide as Sam's hand, the lid screwed tight. Shooting it would have been kinder. She could feel the bend of its wings, the crushed breath.

She wished he'd at least loosen the lid. "Won't it suffocate?" She knew it would. She wrung her fingers.

"Doesn't matter, pin kills it anyway."

"You'll kill it?" Her fingers ceased moving.

"I'm a collector, cases of moths and butterflies under glass. I'm hunting a male."

"To what purpose?"

"To look at, what else. You want to see? You're a Chesterton, right?"

God help her, she did want to see, at the same time hating the thought. "I couldn't," she said. "Not under glass."

"You want this one?" Barth flicked the jar with his fingernail. "Just a female, see, scrawny antennae." He knew moths, but what else was he hunting?

Before he could change his mind, Sam took the jar, unscrewed the lid, shook it gently, and watched the moth unfold with a quick twitch of pale wings and disappear in the dark.

Sam wanted to see their mutual interest in Lepidoptera as likability, his gift of the Luna a kindness to Sam as well as the moth. As a neighbor, he was hers and the Chestertons'. She didn't bother to explain, and she forgot about the man he might have been hunting.

A few weeks later, she met him officially. Sam was about to exercise Lucifer when Barth came by the stable. A fellow in his late teens, she thought, tall, good looking in a soft sort of way, a yellow forelock falling across one eye. No pistol this time.

Sam looped the reins over the paddock rail. "Afternoon," she said and ran a calming hand down the horse's rump. Barth, on foot, closed the space between them.

"Another cup of tea," he said, "and I'd float away." He dropped his eyes and kicked at the dirt. He didn't seem to recognize Sam. "Actually, I got tired of tea party chatter." He looked embarrassed. "I guess Miss Chesterton noticed. She asked if I wanted to see the stable, so here I am." He held out his hand. "Bartholomew Kane." And with an easy smile, "Call me Barth."

"Sam," she said and shook his hand. She'd expected aloofness, but he didn't seem to care about her standing. "You're rebuilding the Biddle place, aren't you?"

"The *Kane* place," he said. Well, a little aloof. Then again, this impression was belied by the intense search of her eyes as if he saw a part of her that she hadn't seen herself, and that *something* stirred. She looked away.

"Giving it a touch of Versailles," he said.

"Oh?" Sam laughed.

Barth looked startled, but continued, "Yeah, big gardens down to the river, a new stable. Fifteen horses coming." As if his palms had gone damp, he rubbed them on his thighs. "Haven't been on a horse lately. I could use a refresher." Self-deprecating. Funny and remarkably friendly—if the rest were like Barth, they'd make good neighbors.

"I'll bring out Sadie. She's big but easy."

"This one's fine," said Barth. With a pat on Lucifer's haunch, he stepped to the horse's side.

Sam raised a warning hand. "Don't…" No time for more, Lucifer slammed his rump against Barth's chest, landing him on his backside, mouth open.

"Roll away." Sam kept her voice as calm as she could.

Lucifer, true to the name, could trample Barth, putting an end to Sam's everything. Without ceremony, Barth by the ankle, she dragged him beyond Lucifer's hooves.

Barth shut his eyes on a sharp look. Pain?

"You all right?" She offered a hand.

He gripped it and hopped to his feet. "Can't keep a Kane down." Still affable. Considering. He smacked dirt off the seat of his once pristine pants.

"Not much for horses, are you?"

"Now that you mention it, no." That look again: deep blues up from under his eyebrows. "You could teach me." He gave her a shy smile.

She found herself wanting to know this person who saw the Samanthos she'd squashed in the bloom of her broadening world. "Sure, I'll teach you," she said, without a thought of unleashing this stranger inside her. Instead, she pondered logistics.

"I'll come when no one's taking your time," he said, his eyes telling her things she couldn't translate. "Wouldn't want to get in anyone's way."

He came late in the day, work winding down, no one else watching his lessons. He learned fast, intent on the proper posture, seeming to want to please. "Is this right? Show me." It was hard to reconcile this young man with Anna's cock-sure classmate.

In a few weeks he came on his own horse, a pale one. A rarity in these parts, this one of the lightest Cremello. "Lots like her," Barth said. "A stable full, soon. Pap's a breeder." This was said more like Anna's braggart Barth. "Scary when you see them at night." He laughed. "Scary as a ghost. Pap's a jokester."

Sam couldn't fathom death-centered jokes; nevertheless, she listened for Barth's pale horse. Its hoof beats at the end of the day triggered an odd lurch in her chest. On those occasional evenings when Barth entered the stable, an unsettling pull drew her to him. An excitement clouded the tasks at hand. A lightness. Tingles in unexpected places.

Until now, she hadn't cared about her hidden Samanthos, even back when her body had begun to change, slight as it was. The tenderness in her breasts annoyed her, forcing her to wear a snug tunic below her loose shirt. Nothing must show. Yet somehow, he'd seen.

Anna had, so why not Barth? And how many others knew and ignored it, Sam fooling no one? A piece of her longed to break out, be the woman she was born to be, but she couldn't give up this other freedom. She shouldn't have to choose.

It didn't matter; she had burrowed deep into the life she wanted, her way opening wider year to year. Though shrouded in fog, more expansion waited, and she didn't need these surges distracting her.

Yet she enjoyed the feelings. And maybe she didn't have to choose. Barth accepted both of her.

She felt light. Lilting, a Luna in flight. Luminous. It seemed Barth felt it too, as his soft hand brushed hers in the passing of a saddle, or shoulder-to-shoulder, brushing Sadie after his lesson.

Days turned to weeks, and she caught him eyeing her, a side-glance in the way that, as a child, she'd eyed the rhubarb pie Mamma set cooling on the windowsill, sweet syrup bubbling through the slits in a buttery crust. Mamma knew how Sam loved it and offered the confection like a hug of approval on a job well done and Sam warmed to the core.

"Thee has to wait," Mamma'd say, her smile affectionate. "After supper." The anticipation would mount as the scent of sweet-tart fruit filled their cottage.

Sam waited for Barth, not knowing her place in this new continuum. Eventually he reached out a hand without the ruse of work. An eager reach. Then... regret?

His yellow forelock fell across one eye hooding a wisp of…
of what? Distaste?

He quickly withdrew, and eyes averted, flicked the hair from
his eyes. So close one minute, shy the next, as if tugged by a
harsher hand than his own.

And finally, his nerve galvanized, he managed a real touch.
Intentional touch.

He overrode his dart-away eyes. They burrowed into hers as
the two of them stood outside the stable door, horses saddled,
their reins dropped, the lesson forgotten. His fingers slid across
hers. Folding them into his, he drew her to his side. His breath
quickened hot on her cheek.

She licked her lips, those lips wanting his, and turned her
head. A wonder, this face-to-face allure.

A puzzlement, too, since kisses came from Mamma at
bedtime, quick lips to her forehead with a hug and admonitions
to have sweet dreams. Paul, never a kiss, lent a helping hand
when she was small, steadying her.

Barth's hand threatened unbalance. His skin to hers sent a
zing up her arm, and this day it traveled from fingers to stomach
to nethers. Curled her toes. A full body zap. Sam shivered, as
if taken with some new sickness. From the side, he eased one
arm around her back, his forearm mashing the knot of his groin
against her hip.

She'd never considered her bodily differences from boys
beyond clothing and her lack of future expectations. When
changing clothes, she drew the bedroom curtain as did Paul.
She never saw him undress or undressed. The curtain stayed
drawn for bathing in the peripatetic tub he lugged bedroom-to-
bedroom and filled with a foot of hot water. Once a week, they
each took a standing bath, including her parents.

For all her curiosity about her four-legged friends, about
millipedes, about centipedes, eight-legged spiders, the articulate
stick-legged beetles, butterflies, moths, it hadn't occurred to her
to equate their rituals to herself. Mamma certainly never spoke
of breeding or birth, not even when Sam's blood started. She just

showed Sam the rags and how to wash them. For all she knew, Father and Paul did the same. The nature of two-legged beasts.

Sure, at night she'd heard raccoons screaming as if tortured in the underbrush. She'd turned her ear to feline caterwauls, seen Lucifer take a mare from behind to prolong the bloodline, a ram humping its ewes and anything else handy. But none shed light on this eye-to-eye, this breath-to-breath enticement.

Her whole body, sensitive as a Luna's antennae, seemed to vibrate. Barth and Sam in a sphere akin to a bubble of soap. They floated amid signals sent and absorbed— such mysterious yearnings. His blue eyes sharpened with hunger. She, his succulent meal, waiting.

He groaned as he rubbed his hardness against her, eyes half-shut, his expression dreamy as if suddenly consumed by a world of his own.

In the slant of evening light, her neck craned, lips just shy of touching his, his other hand sliding over the buttons on her pants, she didn't parse Laz's low nicker, the raise of his head at the trot of advancing hooves. Their beat in time with the throb of her quickening pulse masked the sound. Unheard until the trot turned to thunder, and the roar in her ears became a shout slicing through her confusion, "Bloody hell, boy!" And the bubble burst.

"Father!" Barth staggered backward, hands in the air, his face chalky. Kane's horse skidded to a stop, showering them with dirt. "I'll beat you bloody!"

Barth gave a strangled squeak. "I never..." The lost color returned to his cheeks, cresting at the rims of his ears. With a lurch, he stooped, caught the reins of his grazing horse, and fled. His father, in heated pursuit, thrashed the mare, leaving Sam where she stood, coated in the dust of Barth's all too evident shame.

Oh, shame—But how? How could this wondrous thing, this near touch of lips between a man and a woman, be degrading?

Of course, this could account for Mamma's silence. Sam wanted to ask what made it so—but again, how could she ask?

Mamma dealt with enough shame on Sam's account. She couldn't ask anyone, not even Anna.

These stirrings had confused Sam's focus. She couldn't afford distraction, much less the loss of time that had made her late for home and chores. She'd have to forego this part of herself as she'd foregone all other womanly trappings.

For weeks, shame or not, she listened for Barth's approach, her solitary evenings filled with the low calls of the mourning dove. Just as well she let it go. She would. She'd find a way.

She made herself prod the door shut on this tainted wonder, never for a minute asking how he could see beyond the boy she pretended to be.

A fortnight later, when Sam accompanied Anna home from school, Anna reported on Barth's attentions in class. Always an irritant, his annoyances had now multiplied after his recovery from what he claimed to be a bruising fall—from his horse. A new one, not the pale horse. These were used for "special riders on special occasions," he'd said.

He had the problem animal in hand now. "I used a whip. Taught it a lesson."

On the woods path, Barth appeared for the first time since Sam's bubble burst. He swung the mare in a circle. Stopped before them. "Hi, Anna." Sloppy in the saddle, yellow forelock falling across a purple-shadowed eye, he touched his forehead as if doffing a nonexistent cap.

"Sam," Anna said, "this is Barth. We're in class together." This was said as if she and Sam hadn't discussed him before. Not that Sam had confessed her feelings.

Barth slid a hard-eyed glance across Sam, disdainful and dismissive at once. Wounded, she shrank in the chill and hid behind her everyday-Sam facade.

Barth quickly turned back to Anna. "I'll join you." He circled again, heading now in their direction with Anna in the middle. The three of them walked on together, though it may as well have been two as he entertained Anna with tales of his father's brilliance.

His father hadn't been a subject of conversations with Sam. Nothing of this earth, past or future, had invaded their fleeting moments.

He babbled on, about how west of Pittsburgh his father's laborers mining salt nearly quit, what with black sludge wrecking the take. "But a birdie whispered in Pap's ear," Barth said. "'Back gold.' They sold the oil, and then there was Georgia."

Sam knew there'd been whispers questioning the growth of Kane's Georgia fortune. Another sort of black gold? The signs couldn't be ignored, yet they slid off Kane, the man slick as a mallard's back. They'd have stuck to any other man, mired him thicker than tar under feathers.

Suspicions, yes, but no one seemed willing to declare proof, though a bounty hunt could account for the pistol Barth carried that night in the woods. And more telling: while Chesterton and his ilk lived in diminishing comforts, how else could Kane be flush enough to buy houses on Rittenhouse Square, and in quick succession, the Biddle Estate?

Barth finished expounding on his father's credentials and moved on. "Cook made hummingbird cake," he said. "Come to my house, we'll have tea."

Who makes cake out of hummingbirds?

Anna slid Sam an oh-God glance before answering, "Thanks, no. We have work to do."

"Work? You and him?" He lifted his chin in Sam's direction.

Him—did Barth truly not see the Samanthos inside of her? Could he think Sam was the boy she pretended to be?

She'd rather believe he kept her secret than know him as kin to a ram humping any that crossed his path. She wiped a hand across her offended lips.

"The hunt's coming," Anna said. "We're getting ready."

"I'll be there," Barth said, showing his even teeth in a bright smile. "We'll ride together." He galloped off before she could answer.

Back at the stable, after stripping tack from the horses, Anna and Sam washed them at the trough and toweled them dry. Anna rested her elbows on Caesar's back and said, "Sam, why me? With all those girls to choose from... anyone would love to share his cake." Sam would have. With the other Barth. Not this one.

"So..." Sam swallowed. Keeping it light, she lifted an eyebrow. "It's hummingbird cake you don't like."

Anna threw the towel at Sam's head. She missed. "Barth's fine. A bit too jolly, I guess, always rabbiting from one thing to the next, nothing on his mind. Makes me wonder if he has one."

"He collects insects."

"And that makes him smart?"

"If he studies them." Sam took a pick to Laz's hooves, digging a stone from his right hind frog. Who was this fellow? No hint of the Barth she thought she knew.

"I doubt he studies anything." Anna combed the frayed plating from Caesar's mane. "He's a pest. Worse than ever. In school he sprawls in his chair making jokes. He leans over me, asking for answers, and when I ignore him, he jiggles my paper. The ink smears." She huffs. "He could never be a real friend." She eyed Sam, a trusting look, nothing coy to it or her tone.

Friendship, the simplicity, the depth, a comfort in their silence.

A real friend would warn her. Bury their embarrassment and warn her. "Be careful," Sam said. A warning she should have heeded herself.

CHAPTER 32

SUFFOCATION

When the Kane family had settled into Biddle's newly tarted-up home, Kane Senior, full of ingratiation, sent an embossed card to the Chestertons, among others. "Please join us for dinner."

For the event, Sam drove them in a two-horse trap; Chesterton in gently worn tails, his sister in a fine, full-length muslin, Anna's frock: a bit shorter, simpler. They crowded together, the women's sleeves and skirts fuller than the guests in fashionable attire who disembarked at the pillared entrance. Massive pillars.

For the trip home after dinner, Chesterton sat between Anna and his sister as they sparred across him. Sam, in front on the driver's high seat, pretended not to listen.

"That Kane boy," said Auntie. "So easy on the eyes, he's one to watch."

"I'll leave that to you, Auntie."

"Watch your tongue, young lady. Invitations like this don't grow on trees."

"I expected more neighbors," said Chesterton. "Not an army of… of… the moneyed."

"An impressive group: lawyers, bankers, railroad magnates." His sister patted his knee. "Wouldn't hurt to befriend them."

"I know Johnson in Loans; he's trouble enough. Besides, it's not them—it's the way Kane drops names at their feet. You'd think the Armstrongs were his best friends. Madison and the Monroes, too."

"What makes you think they're not?"

"Please…," he said under his breath.

"And the coloreds?" Anna asked. "Whites did the serving, but in the kitchen…and his stable hands, could they be slaves? And his farmers, the white ones, tenants or not, don't seem to grow anything."

"Foolishness." Sam could hear the purse of Miss Chesterton's lips. "Of course not, not here." In Chesterton House, tenant farmer wives did the cooking and serving at parties. So, who were these coloreds?

"Runaways?" said Anna. "Caught for bounty?"

"Where's this coming from?" Chesterton sounded uneasy.

"School, we studied slavery."

"You see, Ryan, she belongs in Switzerland, not listening to gossip."

Anna's voice came louder, "Auntie, it's not gossip. There's a secret railroad... if Mr. Kane has slaves..."

"Stop this," Miss Chesterton huffed. "He's a good man, very generous. Generous to half the county. We could do worse."

"Mmmm." Chesterton, ever the peacemaker, "I'm sure you're right, Martha."

⁎∾∾⁎

Silence and late-summer heat thickened in the cell. It surrounded Six as if she lived inside a goose down quilt, clogging her nose and ears, sticking to her tongue. On the cot, she squirreled from back to stomach. She gasped for breath.

Sweat pasted skin to skin. She dug at her ears, little fingers, middle fingers. Covered the whole auricle with her palms. Pressed until her head hurt. Couldn't stop the growing fizz. Couldn't shake the relentless claw set in her chest.

The fizz pulsed. She jammed the heels of her hands in her eyes, stars shooting in all directions. If she were roasting on a spit, she'd be well-done by now. Charred by morning.

CHAPTER 33

PRIESTLY VISIT

A fat busybody in black, the priest didn't have to duck coming through her door. Too friendly by half, as if he'd known her all her life. And loved her. "I'm Father Francis." He took her hand. "Call me Father."

Not father of this earth or heavenly, either. She pulled her hands from his. Edge on edge, her teeth grated.

"You must understand," his smile sympathetic, "you're making it hard on yourself. All this tapping and talking."

"What is this tapping? I bumped the wall."

"It's desperation," he said. "The need for another. And that's why I'm here." He sat close beside her on the cot. "To help you confess, redeem you. I've redeemed many." He took both her hands this time. "I'll intercede with God. He wants you…."

The nerve. One more man, this one in lamb's clothing, pretending he has God's ear. That he speaks for God in a language Six can't understand without his all-knowing help.

Her mouth opened. Nothing would spill, gelatinous words stuck in her throat.

"Devil got your tongue?" he said. "Pray with me." He picked up the Bible.

Panic. The letter. Her skinny arm shot for the Bible. "I'll show you what I'm reading." But before she could grab it, the book fell open, the paper floating to the floor. A shot dove. Paul's script looped like a hangman's knot.

"Who gave you this?" No sympathetic smile. No offer of forgiveness from a loving God. "How is this possible?" At least the script couldn't hang Paul.

But Ned. Dear God, she couldn't throw Ned on the priest's mercy. There'd be no mercy for his kindness. She couldn't.

Ned, the one person, a shy rabbit of a person, the one who treated her like a human being. If living in this world meant turning him in, how could she live with herself?

Many days in the dark she'd spun words forward and backward, an agony of conscience that wouldn't come clear. Without lying, what could she say? The Quaker dictum failed to materialize.

Another visit. "Truth," said the priest. "Confide in me, or I've no choice but turn you over to Fergus." The mercy of Rat-Face. "I'm told he's persuasive behind closed doors."

"Yes, and he's why I daren't tell you." How to explain Rat-Face and his threats? "When he's warden, he'll have his way with me. He said so."

"I'm sure you misunderstood. Fergus wouldn't do that. That's not allowed."

Fergus. The man didn't deserve to have a name. "He has a protector. Kane allows him..."

"This is what I mean—you make things harder. Unless you tell the truth, repent, and be contrite, you'll stay here forever." Just what Kane and Rat-Face wanted. No studies. Not even Mamma's brood hen existence. Six's life arranged as if Kane's hands were pulling strings attached to the Rat's hands.

And then, a truth came to her. She'd attach the letter to Rat-Face. "He brought two envelopes, one to himself, one addressed to me. He taunted me with the letter. He said, it's for Sam. Obviously not me, he said, since I was Six. Ned saw him. He can tell you. But it makes no difference. Having told, my life's worth nothing."

"A good start on confession. You accept you're unworthy, not so much as crumbs under the table, yet you've bellied-up to that same table, insisting the supper was yours by right."

"But surely the tortures he..."

"My dear, think of Christ." He patted her hand. "You don't know suffering."

Vengeance
claimed by the Lord
Others in line
Take a number
Why must I
be last

CHAPTER 34

GNAWING

Puddles dry
Unsown pollen rings
depressions green

The letter. All of the guards were called to testify. "Terrified," Ned admitted to Six, along with further talk.

"Ned's a softy," Rat-Face told them. "I bet he did it."

"Naa," Bigger had said. "He's a gutless wonder."

"I'll work on her," the priest said. "Another month with no light, she'll talk."

༄༄

In the dark, Barth haunted Six like a splinter shoved beneath the nails of every finger and toe. Prone on the cot, she rolled her feet in circles. She flexed her knuckles and sank her fingertips into the crunch of the cornhusk mattress. Kicking hard, near silent kicks swam her, a long-distance swim, anywhere away from Barth. Kick-kicking; but his stink filled her cell. He blocked the door and picked at a hangnail. His Pappy sat on the table, legs dangling.

༄༄

In the past, Sam would have loved a day to sleep, the world continuing on without her. Only fever would let it happen. Her income was imperative for the family—what would they do without her, what could they…? STOP. Stop with the questions.

These gnawings dragged Six downriver, a frantic place of nightmares filled with begging bowls, frozen hands in fingerless gloves. Sole-less boots, blackened toes protruding. *Mamma,* cried the shout in her head. *Father.* She'd drown if she didn't rise from the flood.

⁕⁖

Better to stay in the now. But what of Ned? His plight if she told. "Fired?" she'd asked.

"No," he said, "a cell like yours." Treason was rewarded in ways she couldn't imagine. "Be glad you aren't a man." He'd cupped his privates. "I'm begging you."

Another truth to hide. She'd hidden Anna's; silence promised. Sam stayed true to their bond, the depth much greater than that between Ned and Six, yet the consequences—

It felt like life and death for Anna. In fact, for Ned, life wouldn't be an option. The peace of Quaker quiet rang in unending alarm.

⁕⁖

The heating season having come and gone, Sam's muscles throbbed with the memory of lost work. How many seasons had passed without her?

And how many more? Endless years, if Rat-Face had his way. She kicked again, ornery as Lucifer.

"Clarity," he'd laughed. "We have our ways." He pinched the flesh of her arm, his eager squint full of hunger.

Fortunately for Sam, the box of rags by the in-house had sporadic use. As long as she bled, she could avoid his hunger and pretend the threats amounted to noise.

Sleep came slowly.

CHAPTER 35

NOISE

Sam couldn't afford the gift of a morning. Up. Up.

Dawn had not yet pushed across the edge of the earth. She wanted to lie hidden in the half-grown hay, let songs fill her—the peepers' steady throb outdone by tree frogs, out-sung by the glug of the bigger bulls joyfully tonguing at hatchling-gnats in a nearby pond.

A heavy load waited for her fork at the stable. She couldn't make the morning free to listen and watch for catfish. She'd rely on memory replaying the familiar slaps of its tail, how it brought insect songs to an anxious silence, until ripples smoothed and music again rose over bank and field, filling valley to hilltop, enveloping barns and houses where others were kept heedless in weary sleep.

Returning after work, she reveled in the chitter-chitter-chirp of crickets. In grasshoppers sawing wing-on-leg, interrupted by click-beetle clicks, and below them, the thrumming of katydids as they too rubbed their wings, their love song heard by ears on their beloveds' legs. And all the while came the pulsating whine of cicadas, the males making the noise.

Evenings had been that way since she could remember, until Kane arrived, and his laborers came into the forest with their bluster and thunk—the hallmark of men with axes.

And after the alterations on their house had been finished, he'd tasked them to fell the old trees, which they did. Trees with trunks thick as three men together, clear-cut to the river.

With a fury of hacking enough to make a dead man hear, they carved access to Kane's God-given view. Never mind that half the acreage belonged to Chesterton. Oh, the noise.

"Your land?" asked Kane, full of surprise the day Sam drove Chesterton down to confront him. "Why, that's terrible."

Chesterton, out of the carriage, stood dwarfed by pillars of the mansion porch. "Yes, it's a problem."

"An accident, I assure you. I'll have words with my foreman. Do let me pay for the wood. Better still, the land's no use to you—I'll buy it."

Chesterton family land? This sacred land?

Five-hundred acres bought from the man who had bought them from William Penn? No. But Chesterton believed Kane's wistful apology and the unintended nature of his foreman's mistake.

Later, the kindness of Kane's offer to clear stumps impressed everyone, as well as monies loaned to the landed in straightened circumstances. He apologized further as he, Kane, Chesterton, and Sam rode the property, "I owe you for this. Perhaps I could be helpful, since the bank refused your loan." They didn't think to ask him how he had this information.

As promised, Kane had the giant stumps uprooted. He stacked them stiff as petrified spiders, making a barricade against Chesterton's edge of the cleared swath. All access was cut off.

The minions piled on the deadfall, piled on the newly cut limbs with leaves green and withering. The hardwood trunks simply disappeared along with the groundswell of cicadas, the high piping, the peeping and cheeping of secret birds and infinitesimal insects. Or was it just the quiet of advancing winter, as the Kane faithful claimed?

In the silence, Sam prayed the indigenous music would swell again come spring.

CHAPTER 36

FOX HUNT

A cold wind announced the first foxhunt. That year's meet was to be held on the Clay estate, Chesterton's neighbor on the opposite side from Kane. Chesterton, in his pink coat, had gone ahead marshaling the hounds and whippers-in.

Anna and Sam had turned out the horses in their best tack, manes and tails carefully braided, hooves oiled, legs massaged.

The pair rode, parting early mist as it rose from low swales and thinned over the ridges. Excitement hung in the air.

Their horses snorted, twin dragons exhaling smoke, and threw their heads as high as martingales allowed. Ears waggling, they strained at their bits.

Anna twisted on the saddle. "I'm nervous," she said and jerked at the hem of her fitted jacket. "All trussed in black." Folds of her skirts flowed across her knees, the foot of one black boot showing below.

She held the reins one-handed and stuck a gloved finger behind her stock, craned her neck, and pulled. The white tail of the knot dislodged from her vest and she re-tucked it. Her grip on the reins tightened, and Caesar sped up.

Sam preferred Paul's kind of fox hunt, those early mornings when she'd been young. No horses, no hounds. A vixen and her kits only. A skulk of foxes, he called them. Odd, when Sam and Paul were the ones skulking through the grass.

At the base of a hill, "Den," he'd mouthed, and pointed at a clutch of rocks.

They'd stretched on their bellies, feathery grass tickling their noses. Paul flicked her hand, shifted his eyes right, and there was a red vixen, black-tipped ears erect, stepping lightly, not twenty feet off. A leggy mouthful dangled from her jaws. She yipped and soon, from between boulders, fuzzy kits wobbled forth. They bared milk teeth and nipped each other's ears. On spotting her rabbit, they galloped, tripping over out-sized paws.

The kits set teeth into the rabbit's fur, growled and tugged, their lips tinged with blood, but the skin wouldn't tear. Meatless and whining, they attacked one another until the vixen tore the rabbit's belly, spilling an offal feast.

Quiet and joyful, a family moment; not as it was now, perhaps this family about to be hunted by a field of riders hot for blood.

Anna, abreast of Sam again, said, "Must I ride with Barth?"

"You're riding with me, remember?" said Sam. "Your Father's command, and we wouldn't want to counter his command, would we?"

Anna's lips twitched at the corner. "Certainly not." She squirmed and wriggled her knee tighter over the invisible pummel. "I wish Auntie wasn't so bossy."

"Sidesaddle, her subject, or Barth?"

"Both, and other things."

"Like what?"

Anna paused, took a breath, and shook her head. They rode on, Sam slightly forward so that when the words burst out, Anna spoke to Sam's back. "Why should I marry? Auntie never has." She sped up for a face to face. "What's the use of loving Meadowvale, learning the mechanics, then turning it over to someone else?"

Her voice rose. "Worse yet, a know-nothing like Barth." They rode on without a word.

Tree limbs waved across the trail, making them duck their heads. Anna leaned closer to Sam and said, "She's set on him."

"Still?" Sam straightened.

"She asks him to tea and insists I be there."

"Maybe she needs a chaperone." Sam grinned.

"Stop that, I'm serious." Caesar jigged. Funny how horses sense irritation. "I'd never kowtow to him."

"Do you have to? Marry, that is."

"If I found a man like you...." She slapped Sam's knee. "Maybe Paul?"

Talking with Anna had a comfort to it, something deeper than the discussion of books, more sustaining than times with Paul, and with it, some unsaid understanding. Their bond, there and not there when she tried to define it. An acceptance beyond words, beyond facts. Sisterly and sustaining was the best she could do. Too bad people aren't as smart as horses.

"I'll miss you when you go to university," Anna said.

"And I you." More than Sam cared to admit.

"You'll meet so many people in the city, see exciting things; you're bound to fall in love, and that's the way to marry. Being in love."

They picked their way along the boundary between woods and open land. "I'll always love this." Sam opened her arms to the patchwork of fields with stubbled cornstalks rolling alongside the shorn bristles of scythed hay. Hedgerows were dotted yellow and red with fall-bitten leaves, more color speckling the woods.

"I bet you love horse sweat," she said.

"Wholesome and honest, who wouldn't?"

Anna nudged Caesar to a trot. "That's why we get on."

"Seems like Barth wants to do more than 'get on.'" Sam urged Lazarus forward.

"God forbid." Anna shuddered. "He'll become his father."

"Seems likely." The man who nearly trampled Sam without a second glance. The dirt lingered.

"You should see it. His wife keeps a pace behind, and he answers if someone questions her." Anna shooed the image away with her hand.

Sam had seen them stand at their door saying good-bye to the Chestertons. Kane held his wife's arm tight, as if she might run.

"Papa says he's a boot-licker."

"Hasn't licked mine," said Sam.

"He'd rather a banker's boots." She hid a laugh in her elbow. "So why..." looking up, serious this time, "why would Auntie encourage Barth?"

The woods thinned, and through the trees, they saw the Clays' meadow filled with a sea of horses gathered from across the county. Anna put a finger to her lips. "Never repeat. They don't usually talk that way."

And now, with full attention, they entered the group. Everyone's eyes followed the hounds sniffing at the edge of the wood, noses to the ground, eager for the scent of fox.

Sam liked dogs. She loved riding trails and the sight of a red fox sprinting across a field—these the ingredients of riding to hounds and yet she hated this.

She hated the congestion and noise, the strict adherence to flared pants, the strangling stock. At least she could wear tweeds, unlike the gentlemen in black frock coats, though the whippers-in wore pink, dubbed pink despite their jackets' rich scarlet. They wielded six-foot whips, braided leather, a lash at the end. And here Sam was, at the heart of it, the teeming mass of horses turning up clods of turf.

The usual riders waited impatiently. Sam knew faces without names. Then came Barth, cutting unceremoniously through the milling field. His bay horse pressed toward Sam and Anna, and unable to curb the hunter's jigging excitement, he yanked her in a circle. Crowded knee-to-knee with Sam. Barth's crop grazed her thigh, his voice almost inaudible, "Out of the way *poof.*" And smack, Barth cut Laz a sharp blow across the rump. Laz leapt forward. Sam jolted back in the saddle, her eyes smarting.

"Anna, here you are without an escort. Please let me." He gave her a bow and touched the brim of his top hat as Sam reined in. She brought Laz around to Anna's left, keeping to the appointed position, determined to ignore Barth's taunt, whatever it meant. This wasn't the schoolyard, and she wouldn't incite him further. Wither Anna went, Sam would stay close.

Late to the start, another rider broke from the woods, his dark horse at a gallop. Kane. No pale horse. What occasion could be more special than this?

His black hair flew from under a top hat. The horse, unable to cut the crowd, veered around the edge. Kane searched the throng.

All eyes swiveled from the hounds to him, as uninvited, he headed for the whippers-in. He wore a five-button coat, the style appropriate if he were one of their honored group, but Kane's coat glared pink. Pink pale as a young girl's cheek, compared to the proper scarlet. The color called pink after the original tailor, one Mr. Pinque.

Anna put a hand to her mouth and turned her head from Barth. Eyes a-dancing, she squelched a giggle. Though Sam kept her face straight, she joined Anna, grinning within.

Kane raised his whip to Chesterton on the far side of the field. "Tally-ho," he shouted, clearly unaware he just claimed to have seen a fox. His over-long lash dragged the ground. "Hold on, I'm coming."

As Kane approached, Chesterton watched, lips pressed bloodless. Like a second skin, he wore the proper Master of Hounds attire—pink coat, somewhat worn at the cuffs and elbows, flared britches, black boots. He never looked down his nose at the horsemen of his field, but Kane's invasion seemed to test his restraint.

As Kane came within speaking range, the cry of a single hound cut the air. Chesterton wheeled his horse. The rest of the hounds gave tongue. At full cry, they leapt for the woods. Chesterton raised a copper horn to his lips, sounded a pulsing wail, and the field surged for the trees in a red-crested wave.

The meadow drained to a silence Sam wished she could share. She'd have liked to remain behind on the beat-up turf, as she had before accompanying Anna.

Those days, when the baying hounds and hoof beats had faded, it took a few minutes for the shock to ease before a profound quiet took hold. The unpeopled hills rolled before her, the subtlety of meadow-talk filling her ears.

On her own, Sam preferred a cool-down walk along narrow trails or crossing wide meadows. Alone in the quiet, she'd often stop and listen to the wind, its benefit of bird song, the lilting thrush a dusky favorite. In the morning: the gentle call of doves, the yip of fox kits at play.

This time, the field of horses strung ahead in single-file through the woods, with Sam behind Anna, then Barth. They pounded the trail. "'Ware branch," Anna called to Sam. She needn't have worried. Sam rode three lengths back, plenty of time to duck the slap of the next low bough.

Behind, she could feel Barth closing the gap. "'Ware…" Laz gave an annoyed swipe with a hind hoof.

"'Ware yourself." Barth surged past, hindering Sam's view of Anna, and gained on her. Did he think this a race? "'Ware branch," she called again. Instead of ducking, Barth caught the flexible end in his gloved hand. He held for an extra second as if to give Sam space to pass, but in reality, made it impossible. She couldn't get there in time, and slowing pace would put the following rider at risk.

Barth had levered the tension so hard she couldn't tell exactly where the leafy switch would catch her, but catch her it would.

He'd gone beyond chill to intentional hurt, driving the withered remains of Samanthos deep inside.

No time to savor the taste of ash, Sam tucked her head, twisted, and led with her shoulder low over Laz's withers. The branch whipped across her back, its feathery end snapping a circle into her face. A stinging blow. More aggravating than dangerous, the equivalent, had she been a gentleman, of a glove smacked across her cheek. She was no gentleman. Then again, neither was he, much as Barth pretended.

They pounded on into the open relief of another meadow. The riders spread, ready to take one in a series of coops over the property-dividing fence. Anna headed for the highest, pink coats ahead rising in a wave. The pinkest, the last of them, sat off center as his horse took the coop. Both his hands clung to the pummel. His whip fell, startling the horse and it lurched. Kane lost a stirrup.

Repeatedly stabbing at the iron with his toe, he gouged the horse's side, and they sped toward the opposite woods where the hounds had disappeared.

"Go easy," Sam called to Anna. She slowed to a canter.

As if this were a signal, Barth yelled, "I'll show you how." He lashed his horse with a crop. The hunter reared and leapt for the jump. Barth, elbows out, reins high and loose, ignored everything Sam had taught him. Again, he lashed the animal, and crowding ahead of Anna, rushed the fence.

"Anna," Sam shouted, "Hold up." Reins hard on Caesar's neck, Anna gave way as Barth took the jump. The animal's front hooves caught the top rail, and with a clatter, pieces of rail tangled its legs. The horse stumbled, pitching Barth face first on the ridge of its trimmed mane.

Much as Sam disliked etiquette, this demonstrated why the rules of the hunt weren't always arbitrary decrees of stuffy old men too pleased with senseless tradition.

Blood trickled from Barth's nostril. "Clumsy goddamn son of a bitch." He sawed the bit, his horse, neck craned, open-mouthed. Her tongue writhed as the curb dug into her tender palate. One more cruelty in a day full of it. With his sleeve, Barth wiped a swath of red across his cheek—shades of the blooding to come.

Anna and Sam, leaving Barth to collect himself, looked ahead to the center of the field and took an alternate fence. They caught up, but the fox had doubled back, crossing its original line, and split the pack until the whippers-in corralled the strays.

The pack snuffled slowly, outmaneuvered yet again as the fox lost them in a stream, giving everyone a chance to rest before further exploration continued downstream, then up.

The scent finally caught, the cry sounded; the field took off at a gallop. Sam hoped it wasn't one of her friends from last spring's litter.

Well into the late afternoon, horses and riders flagging, it looked like a sightless day, when "Tally-ho," rang for real, and there he was, the fox, head low, slowly cresting a close ridge. Sam prayed the animal would go to ground and stay there.

The sighting rejuvenated hounds and riders alike. They streaked after the benighted creature. Sam didn't want to see what clearly was coming. She sat back in her saddle, light touch on the rein and, with Anna, drifted to the outskirts of the field.

Sam wanted to stop and return to the barn. This couldn't be done without a calamitous reason, plus permission of the Master, though nothing said they had to attend the kill.

Sam could see Kane perilously close to the Master, and Barth closing on the group. If he wasn't careful, he'd interfere with the whippers-in. And maybe that would be good, an unforgivable offence putting an end to the Kanes' charade.

Sam knew the kill would be bad, Anna's heart more tender than Sam's. But the sound, Sam wished she could stop the sound of their quarry at bay, how the hounds would sing. Sing high. Sing ecstatic and lunge.

The scrabble, the snarl, each hound vying for a taste of fox before the whippers-in could call them off, claim the torn body, and give mask, brush and pads to the Master.

A kill to no purpose, Sam sitting helpless against it. She could rebel, but with her influence nil, what good would it do? Maybe Anna, when she'd taken the reins of the family estate, could make a difference.

Sam kept Anna at the opposite end of the field. Hoping to drown out the kill, she talked of the breakfast to follow, the Club Ball that night.

"I'd rather stick pins in my eyes," Anna said. "Barth claims he'll fill my card." In the saddle, she gave a little swagger. "Every dance!" She sighed. "Auntie says, be polite, he's a neighbor. And he's easy on the eye. Hers maybe, not mine. I'd…"

"Anna," Chesterton called as he trotted toward them through the parting crowd. Barth followed closely, his whole face a grinning smear of red. "You missed the blooding," he crowed. "My first kill!"

Chesterton stilled his horse beside Anna. Pride in his eyes, he leaned to her, reaching for her face, in his hand a torn piece of fox, a black strip at the edge of its red fur. "Hold still," he said and drew the bloody skin over her forehead, down each cheek, and dabbed her chin. This was her first kill as well. Sam's gorge rose.

"A virgin no more," Kane shouted from the crowd. "Lucky fox." He laughed.

A dead fox. Sam swallowed her words before they escaped. She felt sick. And beyond sick with thoughts of the ball, how Anna would shiver with revulsion as Barth took her in his arms, pressed himself against her, all sanctioned and in public— she without a voice in the matter. Sam shuddered in her own revulsion. To think that she'd wanted that very attention.

Through the winter, much to Sam's amazement, the Kanes came uninvited to the hunt. At least Barth's father wore regulation pink, though he hadn't the right, and went around glad-handing at every opportunity.

"How is it possible?" Sam asked Anna.

"A mystery." She shrugged. "A father like that; I try to feel sorry for Barth. But I can't."

The noise and confusions of hunt season ended, and Sam spent spring evenings after work, dinner, and dishes, by herself. She walked the upper fields behind the stable, a good place to watch the sunset and mull over her confusions.

One evening, stunned and a bit disturbed, she found Anna doing the same.

"I snuck out," Anna admitted, a little sheepishly. "Please don't tell. Auntie would have a conniption. She'd send me to Switzerland—no more lying in the grass as evening falls."

"Funny, I do the same, and listen to the quiet."

"Oh, I've interrupted. I should go."

'Sisters," Sam said. "Remember."

"I have to remind myself." Anna laughed. "You're not a boy."

"We'll listen together."

"You're sure."

"Yes." And to her surprise, Sam was sure.

She sprawled face up to the approaching dusk, Anna at an angle beside her. As they listened, the quiet filled with the drone of nectar-laden bees returning to the hive. Japanese beetles made lace of leaves in the close hedgerow, and with no sound at all, they watched the float of late migrating butterflies. This heaven was her home, and Anna's sisterly company made it more so.

CHAPTER 37

CONFRONTATION

One evening later that following spring, Kane rode up to Sam's family cottage. No glad-hand extended.

Father, Mamma, and Sam sat at supper, relaxed in the glow of the oil lamp. They worked on first helpings of lamb stew, potatoes, and jarred beans while discussing the day's accomplishments and the morrow's needs.

The evening being fine, the door stood open.

Through the yard gate, they watched a rider steam toward the cottage and rein in by the porch. "Lawson," he demanded. The horse danced in place, mouth foaming. Kane wrestled the animal to a standstill.

Father excused himself from the table and stood in the doorway, napkin in hand. "Mr. Kane?"

The man stood in his stirrups. He looked down on Father. "You can't fail my son."

Father kept his tone even. "I'd rather not, what with graduation near." He stepped into the yard. "Your boy's smart; he could do the work. If he cared. He's missing an essay on slavery, a rewrite. His wasn't to class standards."

"What?" Kane's horse advanced. "Abolitionist standards?" If his words had been dirt, he couldn't have spat harder.

Father retreated to the porch. "My personal point of view is immaterial. I teach history."

Kane sneered. "Horseshit." His mare danced sideways. "I wrote that essay."

"That's unfortunate, and I'm sorry." This was no idle commiseration. Father looked truly unhappy. "So, no credit goes to Barth."

"What's it to *you*?" Kane glared.

"Because," Father bowed his head. "This is where it begins."

"Where what begins?" Kane seemed stumped, a kid at the blackboard confronted with an equation he'd never seen. Then, a growing sunrise took his face, pink to red to purple as if Father had reassembled torn pages of his personal diary.

"This is your fault." Kane extended his chin. "Your mess." Upper lip lifted, he bared his teeth. "It's your job; pass him."

"I warned him," Father said, and tucked the napkin in his pocket. "At this point, I can do nothing."

Kane squinted. "Well, I sure as hell can." With a lash of his quirt, he wheeled the horse around. Clods of dirt flew, and he galloped down the wooded lane.

Father returned to the table, and they all stared at their plates without eating.

The ensuing days unfolded as usual, Barth in school, lounging in his seat, teasing the girls. "For once, he's leaving me be," Anna said as she and Sam rode toward the stable. "Not even a glance at my test."

All seemed well until Friday, two weeks later, when a hand delivered letter arrived:

Dear Mr. Lawson,

I'm sorry to inform you that, by a unanimous vote, your tenure has been terminated as of the end of class this week. A replacement has been assigned for the remainder of the year.

Sincerely,
The Board of Directors

Five signatures followed.

The end of class this week. The day being Friday meant his tenure ceased that very day. Father laid the letter on the supper table at Mamma's place. She read it to herself, and passed it to Sam.

Enveloped in silence, they picked at their meal, knowing that the bitter taste on their tongues had nothing to do with Mamma's cooking. Everyone finished eating, and without a word, they took the dishes to the kitchen pan. Mamma washed, Father and Sam dried.

Wiping the last one, Father said, "In time, all will come clear." Sam wanted to believe, but how long would it take?

They set out tomorrow's plates on the kitchen table, bowls on top for oatmeal, brown sugar in a jar. A creamer waited for cream that at this moment sat rising in the milk house, all efforts made to make the evening whole and unchanged.

Every two weeks thereafter, Sam turned over her wages to Mamma. There'd be no saving for university; not until Father found another school.

To no avail, he walked the surrounding towns. He expanded his circle.

Eventually, he started well before dawn, and still no opening came for this year or next. "Kane's influence?" Father shook his head. No one wanted to think so.

Before dusk one evening, returning from riding the fence-line, Sam and Chesterton met Father on the road home. Father's pace was slow, his shoulders slumped.

Chesterton reined in Lucifer. "You're out late," he said.

"Woodley's a ways away on foot." Father mopped his brow. "Carsonville tomorrow, farther yet."

Chesterton gave him a smile, odd under the circumstances, almost as if he enjoyed Father's predicament. "I can't spare you a horse, but I think you'll like an invention I have." He clicked his tongue, and the horse stepped forward. "It's in my cellar. Come on, double-up with Sam."

Father soothed Laz's rump, leap-frogged behind Sam, and together they followed Chesterton to the rear of his house where they descended the stairs to the cellar. Chesterton lit a candle and guided them to a dark corner. "Cover your ears, Sam."

The candle held out with one hand, he put a conspiratorial arm around Father's shoulder. "One night, after 'a few-too-many'..." He twisted fingers in front of his lips, a locked secret, and nodded to a two-wheeled contraption leaning against the wall. "I bought this thing. 'Our future mode of travel,' the fellow claimed." Chesterton grinned. "That was the end of my taking 'a few-too-many.'" He lifted the thing upright, and Sam, with Father's help, walked it upstairs.

Out in the dusk, Chesterton said, "He called it a velocipede."

"Brother to a millipede? Must be fast."

"Never saw the like again, so who knows."

Father swung a leg over the saddle. "Looks faster than walking." With long strides he wheeled it to the drive's incline and took a wobbly glide down. "My saving grace," he called.

And so it seemed.

CHAPTER 38

GRADUATION

Sam thought that knowing Chesterton meant knowing the highest of men in high places, and she had no qualms accepting his offer to write his alma matter. She enjoyed other invitations he offered as well, attending Anna's graduation being one of them.

Anna's day. A good day. A time to celebrate, and it beat sitting in the trap, though it felt disloyal to be there, Father having been dropped.

For Anna's sake, Sam would flatten her hackles. Anna had done her best. She'd complained to her papa after Father's first absent Monday—"The new man has mush for brains; he can't control the class. Barth went beyond pest to pestilential."

Chesterton talked to other neighbors who listened politely, assuring him this was the Board's responsibility; nothing more they could say. What's done was done.

He wrote questioning letters to the Board. They went unanswered. His letters grew an edge and cut nothing, all lost at the bottom of some well. No splash. No ripples.

"Surely the Board had good reason," Miss Chesterton insisted.

"Such as?" Anna had asked.

"They'd never gossip," Auntie had reassured her. "Too circumspect."

"I want reasons, Papa told me, not gossip." Others allowed that it must be serious to be so secret. "All five members agreed. They couldn't be wrong, so stop worrying."

On graduation day, Sam donned her tweed jacket, dark pants, jodhpur boots— driving clothes, be it to the village for groceries, taking the Chestertons to church, or dinner at a neighbor's. There were certain expectations Sam adhered to, and this day was no different.

"Join us," Chesterton said. "You're at the reins, so come to the ceremony.

Sam liked the way he blurred the line most owners held sacred. He treated Sam as more than a servant, though not quite a friend.

Miss Chesterton took no part in the invitation. Choosing her battles, Sam supposed. The woman looked the opposite direction and lifted her chin. Anna ignored the distinction and her aunt.

It was a perfect day for an outdoor event. Sam drove the Chestertons in their open buggy. She parked close, and they ambled to a field in front of the stone schoolhouse.

An extravagance of new straight-backed chairs had been set in two sections facing a podium. The Chestertons slid into a row halfway back. Sam took the aisle seat.

The elder Kane's bravado swelled from the front row before he came into view, "...handmade in Philadelphia, cost an arm and two legs, but nothing's too good for my boy's school." He stood as the School Board filed in.

He hailed each man by name, his eyes pinched to slits above an expansive grin. He doffed his top hat, boot-blacked hair combed slick, and shook each man's hand, his face jowly, wattles like a rooster.

All the seats filled, laudatory speeches ensued, and the presentation of diplomas began. Anna accepted hers with a shy bend of her head, while the new teacher bestowed high honors on top. Everyone clapped. Chesterton took his sister's hand. Heads tipped toward one another, they smiled—shared pride warm as the day.

The teacher worked through the alphabet and, coming to K, he announced Barth's name. Kane jumped from his chair, arms waving. "That's my boy!" He clapped wildly. His wife in her seat patted her hands together, sedate, even a bit subdued. Kane made up for her reticence.

Chesterton leaned to Sam's ear. "What, no honors?" It seemed influence had its limits.

The final remarks ended, and the students filed out. Everyone stood and turned to watch the line pass. Barth, in cap and gown, yellow hair falling in his eyes, came abreast of Sam and turned to the boy behind him in line. He grinned. "Did you see Sam's pappy this morning? He rides a hobby-horse." With a smirk, Barth mimicked holding wobbly handlebars. "Can't afford a real horse, not now."

Sam stood rigid in the face of Barth's jab, her jaw clenched. His spoken message was bad enough, but what of the silent one? A secret something that the boys shared. A tale near dripping off their tongues.

Their knowing leers wheedled at her, something so delicious they had to hold it a little longer, savor it, though it badgered to get out. Whatever it was, it was clearly something to dread.

The seed of it stuck in Sam's craw. Rooted, it would grow weedy in heated moments, watered with resentment, nurtured by happenstance. Or had it, whatever it was, been planned from the start?

"Easy there." Chesterton pressed against her shoulder. "Don't make it worse."

CHAPTER 39

GREEN PLANT

*A slice of sun
The unimagined in waiting*

Retribution: Rat-Face in a slow burn. Six could feel his heat through the walls, fire apt to burst out at any moment. He'd sear her—to the soul if he had his way.

So far, he'd inflicted no scars she could touch with her fingers, yet helplessness scorched within.

"Investigation." Ned told her, his hushed voice over her shoulder, the day he surprised her with yard-time. "Looking into Tall-Boy and Bigger," he whispered.

Father Francis had caught them lurking at her door. He'd made the yard happen, citing that a respite could break her resistance more surely than continued darkness. "If it doesn't work, you can count on a ducking." His voice hushed further, "Maybe the mad chair. Enjoy the yard while you have it."

Enjoy—would that ever be possible? He locked the outer door, and she worked to blot out the Rat's possible reprisals. She paced uneven ground. Think green.

Despite having studied every inch of the yard before, she scanned for green between bits of chiseled block never cleared after construction. How many summers had she done this? Yet every time it looked different.

Earth below the rubble called her fingers. The desire to plant and tend and gather, so deep-seated from a lifetime of summers beside Mamma in their garden. The earth offered something new to look forward to every day. Their reward—sustenance through the winter. Six's reward—another world where she'd roam.

More green—a need she hadn't anticipated. Hadn't thought it could be so strong. A kind of loneliness, sharp as the absence of touch, the lack of kind words.

Her attempt to find a hint of anything growing proved fruitless until, at one corner touched by a glimpse of sun, hope quickened. Grass had once grown there, telltale strands poking brown from behind a chunk of stone. She pushed the stone aside and swept at the gravel, tore matted thatch, and unearthed an anemic little shoot. Unable to pierce the sodden thatch, its wry neck had bent, head forced to return to the earth.

She carefully scraped a circle around it, clearing down to loam, and the shoot, she could swear, straightened ever so slightly. Its joy in the sunlight ached in her chest. She knew the crink it felt, those hours crouched below the skylight, straining to see a slice of sun that never came. But here, she had it for minutes on end, and now this foundling had sun too.

Every day her waif grew, from dead pale to a green tinge. It unfurled a tiny leaf, round and veined. Another joined it. She wanted to spend precious outside time beside it. Coddle it. Wanted to clear the entire area surrounding it. Wanted to make a farm where it could flourish. The blessing here: no slugs to feast on her waif's infant tenderness.

Years ago, Sam's garden had been infested until Mamma learned about salt.

Sam cringed when Mamma sprinkled the slugs. A fine coating of crystals made them shrivel in a pool of their own secretions. Sam had turned away.

After a season of this, Paul rescued Sam. He said that the slugs would die happy, drowning in ale. Mamma wouldn't allow it in the cottage, so Paul slid jugs behind the grain bin, set out pans at night, and full by morning, Sam emptied the bloated bodies behind the barn.

Six had visions of her waif's little green friends rising from the earth. These brought a garden dancing in her head, heart-leaf beans, feathery carrot tops, the crawl of squash and cucumber, red legged beets, heads of curly lettuce.

Real vegetables. She couldn't tell what her mush-filled bowl contained. The loaf on her plate couldn't be recognized either, both cooked gray and tasteless.

Reading the Bible, and with an hour in the glory of the yard, she settled into a rhythm. The priest, her protector, snuck under her skin with kindness. She could only be grateful.

At first, glad of a person in her cell, she could ignore his nattering. His regular visits softened her resistance, though not enough to call him Father. Never.

He pressed for her sins, and undercurrents surfaced. "Holding your tongue has to cease."

The story of a letter had failed, Rat-Face admitting his taunt. He swore he'd burnt that letter. Testimony accepted, the attention returned to Six.

The priest, "A name, a name." He pricked Six to full resistance. "At Cherry Hill we maintain order, and truth is key." Both things she believed in, though no truth would bring order. Not here.

He wore his kindest smile. "Help me to help you." Sincerity oozed. "A name. Please, I can't hold them off forever." He shuffled to the door. "You know their methods." She didn't, not really. "There's not much time, please."

Time. She'd had nothing but time. And now it's short? She saw his words for what they were—matches he struck to ignite her. Their flash burned her; her only refuge was found in the yard where she could lose sight of her other surroundings.

Blessing the light, she coddled the green waif as it grew. Her feelings of purpose, of accomplishment, were restored, small as they were.

By habit she kept her back to the distant tower and blocked the view of a guard who couldn't be seen. She wouldn't risk cultivating an entire home for her foundling and contented herself with scattering dry grass over the surrounding earth instead.

Necessity kept her striding corner-to-corner of the yard. She squatted here and there to distract the guard, and if he noticed her excessive attachment to this one spot, she hoped he wouldn't know the joy her green dependent brought day after day.

The infant stem leafed out. Now tall as her ankle and coltish in its struggle, it stood firm. Scalloped leaves grew lush in youthful promise, and under them, nestled in their protection, a pink swelling emerged. Six's treasured foundling had come into bud.

In her excitement she jumped up with a quick dance. She wanted to spin, but stopped. She suppressed bubbling laughter.

Was this how her grandmother felt when Mamma's belly swelled beneath the folds of her gray skirts?

With a sidelong glance at the tower, she sprinted to the opposite wall and knelt, heart beating fast, forehead pressed to the corner. She prayed the guard hadn't been looking.

The bloom—a living, breathing, being—radiant, its face turned to the sun. Six hugged herself.

> *Cauldron grown this bud*
> *my green and saving grace*

CHAPTER 40

THE ACCIDENT

After graduation, Anna's father and aunt collected her. Sam drove them home, stomach roiling. Her glasses slid on a sheen of sweat, and she shoved them against the bridge of her nose.

In no mood to celebrate, she took herself to the stable and shoveled manure until suppertime neared, and then walked the road toward home. Hard work hadn't quelled the irritation. She kicked at loose stones, bouncing them off the road until one stone glanced off her boot, skittered over the verge, and into a ravine.

Up floated a groan. "The voice barely audible, "Someone, pl…." And it faded.

Sam ran to the verge and peered into the rock-strewn gully. A body sprawled at the bottom in the shatter of wood wheels, the velocipede in smithereens.

"Father!" Sam took the rock bank in great leaps, eyes jumping from her footing to a gash on his forehead, the painful twist of his face. His lower leg cocked where no joint allowed. "Oh Father." She had to….

If only she could cleave herself in two. One of her could stay, hold his hand, while the other ran.

On her knees, she slid pieces of wheel from beneath his spine, shoved rocks, and evened the ground. "What happened?"

His eyes pleaded. His lips formed words, yet no sound. She had to do more, and quickly. She'd seen the method in Father's bone-book, and once while helping Mamma splint a sheep. Bones are bones, she hoped.

His hand inched along the ground toward hers. She held it and bent close. "Your leg needs be straightened." Her eyes welled.

And what then? She couldn't manage the bank. Dear God, help.

Moving slowly, she lifted his pant leg. Skin stretched thin over the break, bone sharp below the surface. God, she prayed, don't make it worse. "This'll hurt."

She placed both hands on the ankle. He tensed.

She tensed. Her face mirrored his pain as she lifted his foot. Father screamed. His body went limp.

Beneath her hand, she felt the rise and fall of his chest. "Thank God."

Back at the ankle, two-handed, she pulled a slowly increasing pressure. The bend eased with a sickening crunch. She aligned his legs and blocked them with rocks. "I'll be right back."

With Chesterton's house the closest, she ran.

She returned with the gardener dragging a cart topped with a plank. The cart left on the verge, they slid down the bank, laid the board next to Father. In and out of consciousness, he groaned as Sam moved the rocks. She tucked the board under his hip and, lifting both legs just enough, pulled him on top.

"Upper end," she said. "You start." The gardener dug his heels into the bank and went up backward, step by step, the board at waist level. The plank tilted. Before Father could slide, Sam raised her end to her chest. More tilt. She lifted to her chin. Feet blind, they felt for purchase.

The gardener crested the bank, and Sam pushed the plank higher. Her arms shook. She staggered, the board tipping sideways. "No," she cried, grunting with effort. Her muscles about to give, she rushed the last steps to the road. Father yelped as the board landed on the cart.

Down the dirt track, the gardener pushed the cart by its handle. Sam walked alongside, Father's hand in hers. She kept the pace slow, and still Father gasped at every lurch. The big wheels jounced the long road home.

At the cottage, the gardener ran for Doc, while Sam and Mamma shifted Father to the bedding they had hastily arranged on the living room floor. "What happened?" Mamma asked.

"An accident." Father's jaw tightened. "Horsemen…." He ran out of breath. They waited. "Didn't see…."

"Hobbyhorse" echoed in Sam's head, the memory of smirk. "Barth," she said, "wasn't it?"

"Between..." he whispered, "us."

"No," Mamma said. "He can't get away with *this*. If you won't, I will."

Panic bested Father's pain. He raised himself on one elbow. "You'll be... a scold, gagged..." Kane would accuse her.

The gag, no simple cloth muffling speech. Sam's hand went to her mouth.

If Kane labeled her a scold, she'd be sent to prison. They'd slip a metal bar like a horse's bit in her mouth, a metal plate attached to the bar's center. They'd hook chains to the ends and lock them at the back of her neck, then attach more chains holding her arms behind her back, wrists yanked upward. More chains would attach to the bit, and with every breath a metal plate would lacerate her tongue.

"No witness... Auburn for you," said Father, his pain overlaid with anger. "Remember the Nation...." The Cherokee Nation; they all knew what he meant, Father ever obsessed with this injustice. Like the Indians, the family would have their own Vale of Tears. Father slumped back on the bedding.

No one but he talked of the Cherokees, so far away and hard to believe. But Auburn, that was real, the prison close as New York. The industrial buildings were meant for men—there women packed attics, all ages and crimes crowded without activity or access outside; flogging and the gag but two of the disciplines. The thought would make any woman hesitate to speak. Without a witness, the man was always believed.

CHAPTER 41

WILLA

I believed Rat-Face. Believed each threat. And had I been with Six as he starved her, I'd have pushed her to swallow every questionable spoonful. Six, like me, her skin thin, dry paper wrinkled over bone.

Eat, I pushed her, but she couldn't hear me yet. Food would be the keeper of her menses. Rat-Face would be kept at bay. Six's only weapon.

Bigger and Tall-Boy ogled her through the bars of the yard door. Sniggered. Plans whispered, the two of them annoyed that their turns would come second and third. The Rat prefers his women unsullied.

CHAPTER 42

GREEN PLANT

Arms to heaven
these arms
but bone and skin
won't lift me winged

Ned opened the door, rousing Six fresh from Sam's greening fields. "Yard time." His face was pale and drawn, though she didn't notice the change, consumed as she was with thoughts of her infant.

Off the cot she dashed for the door, a piece of her still in Sam's world, forgetting the ritual hood, the need of escort across the sill. In her hurry Six bumped past Ned as she would have passed Paul and taken his sleeve to bring him along. Dependent as they were on each other, Six and Ned, certain customs remained in place.

"Six!"

Mid-step, she halted. Afraid to talk or touch him again, for who might see. She bowed in silent remorse, all the while desperate to tell of her foundling. Or silently, she could show him.

Telling would be better. Just seeing, he wouldn't know how it grew, the leaves brushing her cheek as she sat beside it, and now, miraculous in this place of never-ending sameness, a bloom.

"The hood, Six, what's your hurry?"

"I…" she started. He slid it on, snagging the mole on her ear as usual. Her breath ricocheted inside the cloth, a warning shot, and silent, she stumbled toward the door. She wanted to ask if her budding miracle still graced the yard. She had to know, be prepared to see it brutalized.

"Smart," he said. "Watch yourself… as you do me." He sounded a little unsure of the last part. Wistful, almost pleading, his limp pronounced as they lurched outside, Ned as dependent as her green foundling.

The second the outer door shut, she whipped off the hood and ran for the corner, Ned and her promise lost to her singular thought. And yes, her baby lived, green leaves sheltering the blossom. No bigger than her thumbnail, delicate pink, petals open to her smile, as it would open to the sun, and she in turn knelt before it the way others knelt at a shrine.

No attention paid to her rough pants, their chafe at the back of her knees, she rolled the baggy shirtsleeves to her forearms and reached toward the flower, cupped her hands around the aura, afraid to touch her newborn.

Examining every crease and fold, she marveled at the downy calyx, bowl-like, holding the petals, their fragile-pink veined purple. At the center, the tiny pistil stood erect, its dark violet surrounded by reddish anthers.

She breathed in the flower's nascent aroma, the sun warm at her back. Her eyes misted. In the past, she believed she knew this feeling, her heart overflowing, those wee-hour-nights cradling a new foal, but compared to this, on those nights, she'd known nothing. Absolutely nothing.

Her shoulders shook with a stifled laugh. Tears slid down her cheeks, her heart rich with ridiculous joy.

That night, she dreamed a profusion of flowers bloomed around her spool bed. They lifted her, holding her as the calyx held her flower.

They rocked her drowsy through sun-filled afternoons, and the downy hairs grew long. Their delicate tendrils circled her arms. They wound her legs in loving embrace and, reaching for the sun, circled her; the flowers, the sun, and Six, cocooned.

And cocooned tighter, the hairs gone wiry, they squeezed. Squeezed until the sun bled to a shadow of itself.

In the dusk of her morning cell, she fought the dream's constriction, its grip on her innards. She choked on breakfast, a spoonful of mush forced through gates all but locked against it. Two bites were all she could manage, sitting on the cot. As the mush congealed, she wondered if her mother had fears beyond Sam's un-marriageable situation. Perhaps she had an inkling of how Sam would twist into Six, Mamma's dreams of grandchildren crushed beyond redemption.

"Yard time." Ned, in full view, rested his foot on the sill. "Your priest is still hopeful."

"He's not my priest." The man was hardly a person behind his pretenses.

"Shhh, shhhh." He hooded her. "Don't ruin it." He guided her out and shut the door.

Six wandered about her patch of yard. She kept unfocused until she couldn't stay away another minute, her pink infant waiting in the corner.

Her dream was just that. Nothing to fear.

She sidled to the corner and knelt. With her face close to the glowing green, she whispered endearments threaded with future projections, of life rich in fruitful germinations. She admonished it not to mind the clouds, how they brought much-needed rain, and...

"Who you talking to, Cutie?"

So taken with her infant, she'd missed the rasp of the outer door. She'd missed the stealthy shush of Rat-Face behind her, his sock-covered boots now against her back-turned toes, the lilt of his funning sharp.

She stilled, her body a shield, and ransacked her brain for a foxy distraction. A welling of gibbered nonsense flooded her—nothing she could use, even if words were allowed.

A shadow fell: his body, as he leaned over her. "Ooooo, you got a little friend there?" He pressed his knees into her back, and his disembodied hand reached over her shoulder. Weight through his knees forced her onto her hands, his fingers twisting her hair, her face pressed close to the bloom. Her glasses tilted.

The green infant trembled under her frantic breath as the fingers of his other hand closed on the stem.

CHAPTER 43

LAZARUS REJECTED

"No, please." And so similar it was to Sam fighting for the colt. Sam, at fourteen, on her knees in Georgia's stall. Sam hanging onto Jake's arm. "Please, let me keep him."

The last bite of winter hung in the air that morning. Paul and Sam, who by then was his right hand, had rolled open the great stable door. They both breathed in the sweet animal warmth.

One after another, six horses poked their heads over the stall doors. Chesterton had sold off three, cutting expenses.

But the mare, Georgia, didn't show her head. Paul walked the cobbled alley, a quick stroke to each horse's nose on the right-hand side. Sam took the left, keeping to the daily routine despite a growing sense of unease. Their eyes never quit Georgia's vacant door.

Paul pulled on the bolt. The door swung. "Oh God, get Jake."

In the box stall, Georgia, lying on her side, panted. By her rump, her foal, not due for weeks, stretched flat and wet on the straw. Sam ran for the tack room.

If Jake was at the stable, he'd be in his over-stuffed chair, sleeping off the previous evening's indulgence. And there he was, snoring noisily. Sam tapped his shoulder. The snoring continued.

She poked. Nothing. She prodded with the heels of both hands.

"Go 'way."

She pulled his arm. "Georgia's foal... we have to save it."

"Damn."

In the stall, Jake folded onto one unsteady knee. "Oh, hell, it's a colt." They'd been counting on raising a stud, the savior of Georgia's line and Chesterton's reputation as a breeder. This would have been the stallion they wanted, but no longer.

Sam cleared the foal's ears, Paul having seen to its mouth and nostrils first.

"A waste." Jake heaved to his feet. "Worthless, alive or dead." He bent and lifted the foal by one rear hock. The head and shoulder dragged on the straw. "Here." He pushed the body at Paul. "Bone pile."

"No!" Sam caught the foal's head. "You can't let it die." She cradled its neck and withers, taking the weight off the one leg. Her pleading look lost on Jake, she turned to Paul.

"Softest heart in the county," said Paul with a wry shake of his head. He tucked an arm under the foal's chest, one around his rump, and held it. Its legs dangled.

Jake spat in the straw. "Stupid."

"Let me try." Sam clung onto Jake's arm. "Why not? He means nothing to you!"

She and Paul brought the foal home in a cart and carried the limp thing to the darkest corner of their kitchen. Paul laid it on a pile of burlap sacks, the animal a near motionless collection of knob and bone wrapped in a hide covered with wet brown hair. The infant folded in on itself, hooves gelatinous, head too large for its flimsy neck. Ears, longer than a mule, flopped at odd angles. Dark protruding orbs for eyes blink-blinked, the smallest sign of life, and not a good one. Black hairs sprouted from its stubby tail.

She took a towel warmed by the fire, and down on both knees, rubbed the cold from its frail body. Gently, gently, she stroked over washer-board ribs, rubbed his chest, rubbed his oddly domed forehead and down his neck. His blinking eased.

"He needs rest," Paul said as he left for the stable. "Don't let him stand—legs are the last to harden." He knew so much, and more was to come at the university. She needed that knowledge now; so helpless without it. She laid her hands on his side.

The colt's shallow breaths came with such labor. Standing seemed last on the little thing's mind. He hadn't even the strength to lift his head.

She spread a freshly warmed towel over his bones and curled around him, her chest and belly to the knots of his spine. Tig-two purred, her paws caressing the opposite end of the towel.

Through the morning Sam kept reheating towels, and as the foal warmed, his legs shifted. He tried to lift his head.

Lips, once flaccid, appeared to firm enough to suckle. She'd give it a try.

When bringing the foal, Paul had tucked an empty liniment bottle under his arm. "Sam," he'd said, "wash it well."

She did, and following Mamma's instruction, using a funnel, filled half the bottle with cow's milk, dripped honey in the neck, and topped it with water. She swirled the liquid until the honey dissolved and tied a piece of cloth over the top. Long and loose, the cloth, with a few holes in the center, made for a limp teat. She set the bottle on the hearth.

Once the bottle warmed, Sam drew the foal into her lap, its head supported in the crook of her arm. She inserted the cloth into his mouth. He didn't suckle.

Frantic to entice hunger, she let milk leak on the foal's tongue, carefully keeping his mouth below his eye-level. She knew from feeding orphaned kittens how easily, with the best of intentions, she could drown them. Fortunately, they'd sneezed out the milk, her guilt limited to their mewling discomfort. Tig-two lapped the foal's drips before they disappeared in the towel.

Love for this foal already lodged deep, she held him close and rocked. He had to eat. The purring cat gave the foal's nose an encouraging butt.

"Sam?" Mamma's tone said, "pay attention." "Thy chores first."

"But he's starving."

"And next winter... Who starves then?"

They might go hungry if she didn't attend to her work, foremost on the list being planting seeds in the inside boxes: a head start for tomatoes, sweet potatoes, broccoli.

She retrieved a shovel and bucket from the toolshed. Behind their barn she mixed well-seasoned manure and earth, brought it to the house, filled boxes, and hurried back to the foal. Mamma frowned as she peeled potatoes for dinner.

The foal wouldn't suckle then, or an hour later when Sam made another try. "Come on Lazarus, make an effort."

"Oh, Sam." Mamma sighed. "Don't give it a name."

And Lazarus did blossom; the chance her foundling flower deserved.

But no, now, the Rat's steely fingers closed on her plant's green stem. She shut her eyes against the pinch. A curtain of darkness, akin to a covered skylight, couldn't stop the scent of freshly disturbed earth that filtered through, his actions made clear.

Without sight, she knew the dangle of tender roots, the striving leaves. She felt the cock of his arm. The throw. The motion spoke to her through his knees, the lurch against her back as good as showing her infant's trajectory.

She saw it airborne, the leaves collapsed, delicate petals in flight, how one dropped the way Mamma's cut flowers dropped petal by petal. She heard her blossom, soundless as it hit the rock-stern ground, and knew how, over unattended hours, it would wilt—no rebirth possible.

A boiling filled her belly. It expanded bowel to brain, a primitive part of her rising, and before it exploded red behind the eyes, she saw something worse than a blacked skylight coming.

She saw the endlessness. Biting her tongue, she dug fingernails deep into the earth. Her every muscle clamped against the need to uproot the part of Rat-Face she could reach, pull it from his body and dangle it from the highest tower. As if she could ever scale that fortress.

He kept a stiff-armed grip on her neck and shoulder. Deep and personal, his hate lanced through his knees, pierced her back, as if she'd stolen *his* prized possession. Six, the cause of some great loss. If only.

What she wouldn't give to have such power, to crush this rat as he crushed her now. Muscle against muscle, blood beating behind her eyes. Her resistance matched his hate; in her throat a high keening.

And if by some fluke she proved stronger, what then but more hate? Retaliation waiting, its bloated carcass filling her cell. This, like a sliver of self-preservation, cut her. Hamstrung, she crumpled, her face forced into the dirt. Glasses smashed.

CHAPTER 44

TAPPING

Meat in a stone cauldron
hear me bubble
Hear me squeak

Sleep wouldn't come. The hours droned on, silence thick as toffee. Six thrashed just to hear the swish of her blanket.

She flung her legs straight, levered them in the air, and beetled a dance with her heels. She knocked them together with the greatest caution, but not enough, and one hit the wall.

She shrank flat and held her breath. Rat-Face could be out there awaiting a signal. The time ripe for his turn.

Lifting her head off shoes used as a pillow, she listened. She reached for foxy hearing. Cock of an upright ear. Catch the Rat's sock-covered boots.

Hunting for the faintest sound, she shifted her head. He could be listening through her food slot. Bigger and Tall-Boy sliding her door.

Her head tilted an ear toward the wall, shifted back and forth. In passing over the stone, she heard it. The sound was too hard to pin down. A person, please.

Four-legged rats in the pipes. Her anticipation faded.

But again. The tap. Was this the tapping they talked of? The tap scratched, barely a whiff of sound, yet at the same time a whole conversation. Another someone in her situation, there in the midnight-alone. On the other side of the wall—a person. Close enough to talk with. If only she and they had language.

Risky as it was, she couldn't not tap in return. She couldn't leave them.

She wanted to smash the wall. She wanted to feel the flesh of a hand, and hug them, or at least let them know that she knew they existed. That she existed.

No, no, no, she mustn't. Ned was a person, she told herself. The priest. They must suffice.

Up on her knees on the cot, she rested her hands against the wall. Don't do it.

With her right forefinger, she tapped a silent litany that even she couldn't hear. Then, increasing the pressure, she tapped a little harder and a little harder with the soft pad of her middle finger until the sound of soft raindrops talked to the wall. Through the wall. Yes?

She held her breath. Ears pricked, she waited, muscles taught, straining for the slightest return.

The silence hissed. She couldn't hear past it, and reamed little fingers in her ears, twisting a windstorm to blow it away.

More silence settled around her. There'd never been a tap.

Surely, her own fevered imagination. She stopped straining. Slumped limp on the cot. Defeated, and...

And there it was. Through the hissing silence. She heard it.

Something metallic. Three soft taps! She jumped to her feet on the mattress. Ear to the wall. No, not the wall.

They spoke from the pipe, yes. Up from the pipe!

The cot wobbled, and off she hopped. "Oh!" burst from her mouth. "Oh, my God!" So bold, as if unused to repercussions, she fell on the grate, her eye to a hole, peering into the unrevealing depths. "Are you there?" she whispered.

No answer.

Someone escaping wouldn't.

"Please be there." She put her mouth to the grate. "Please."

"Shhh!" came from the depths. "Say nothing."

Sound mushroomed into the cell and ran up the shaft to the dark skylight. "You are there!" A person.

It felt like a lantern in the dark, a shimmer disclosing no walls, no stone floor, a light like the moon soft on the river. She could hear water lap the bank, smell the grass beneath her knees as she knelt for a midnight drink, two hands cupped. An assignation imminent. And then, she heard the door click.

CHAPTER 45

GAGGED

A day the devil devised
time invisible
But when I'm blind
she carries me
Willa the keeper
of what was me

Six leapt to the cot, and crouching, hammered the wall. She'd lead them astray—stagger the opposite direction from her person. Her person was more sacred than a nest of kits.

The inside door shot open. Lantern foremost, Rat-Face stepped in. Bigger and Tall-Boy barged after. No Ned to sound the alarm. Where was he?

They rushed her. My God.

And where was God? Stuck in the chimney with Santa Claus—inanities played their own foxy trick on Six. Stop it.

She yelled, "Hello?" She couldn't lose that disembodied voice, yet she wouldn't hurt them for the world. Her person had to know that she cared.

They'd hang her as a goat instead of a sheep—so what. To hell with the yard; it didn't matter.

"Hellooo!" To hell with the skylight. Nothing mattered but the person. "Hello, hello."

"There's no one there," said Rat-Face. Snide enjoyment played on his face. "That cell's empty." And they fell on her, Rat-Face, Bigger, Tall-Boy. Their multiple hands grappled her hydra of legs, of flailing arms. They hauled her off the cot.

Bigger pinned her against the wall while Tall-Boy crammed a cloth in her mouth and yanked on the hood.

Her world dark, Bigger locked her head against his body. Her ear stung, the mole torn afresh. Boots shushed. He stumbled her through the yard and out to the great beyond.

A long slog and back inside somewhere—Satan's own home? She'd made this happen, that person more necessary to her than her own life. It seemed so. Then.

And now? Was her life forfeit to an impulse? Possibly, her person not even real. Impulse dissolved in the hood's black interior. Her knees gave; her body a drag on Bigger's arms.

He let go of her head, and hands on her shoulders forced her onto those wobbly knees. Off came the hood and before her stood the three guards.

They stood, legs spread, their faces lit from below by a lamp on the floor, giving their skin a ghostly aura. The undersides of their noses were bright, their nostrils dark holes, their eye sockets black, their eyebrows alive with the look of hairy caterpillars.

"You and your mailman," said Rat-Face. He wagged a finger at her. "That's bad enough, but tapping…." Tall-Boy beside him swung a metal bit, square plate in the middle, small chains attached at either end. Bigger held lengths of heavier chain.

She knew of the gag. Father had described it. The thing they used at Auburn.

A threat. Only a threat. They wouldn't use it here.

"Save yourself," said Rat-Face. "We'll forget the tapping, just name your mailman."

Mouth dry, her tongue stuck to her palate ridges. Yes, there's knowing, and then there's the known. The bit dangled before her.

Not yet in her mouth, and she could taste it. "Please, no."

And what they'd do to Ned would be worse. Kindness was his only crime.

But the gag… She couldn't.

She bolted for the door.

Every sinew stretched in her reach for the latch. She hooked the handle, and from behind, calipering arms locked her middle. Lifted her. Her legs ran through the air.

"You don't want to leave," said Bigger. He pried at her fingers. "Not now."

This day, she'd lost the person in her cell. She couldn't lose Ned.

The Devil she didn't believe in shadowed the blackening world. She saw him with her fingers and toes, his touch on her skin, in her innards and outards, in her ears. His scent in her nose.

The walls closed in. Shadow flooded her head. Heavy, the scent of lime. The stink of what it covered. Warm and slippery, her bowels loosened.

And I am beside myself

CHAPTER 46

WILLA

Birthed full grown from an iron canal

Above my head, I scratched at the mortar holding the grate. Dawn and dark and dawn and dark ran together. In the pipe my arms had grown weak, the scraping stone worn to a sliver. Fingers raw. Thirst drove me on, and I shoved the grate with the heels of my hands—the grinding sound of metal on stone. One more shove and the grate lifted. I set it aside and climbed, slick as a sewer rat, into her empty cell.

At the same moment, voices came from the yard, and I squirmed quick as that same rat under her cot.

"…yeah, a bleeder," one said. The blanket hung inches off the floor, letting me see only wool-covered boots. They shuffled, and Six's body dropped belly down on the cot. An arm dangled close at my face.

"…her own blood, she could'a drowned."

"But she didn't," said Rat-Face.

"One more death, your neck's in a noose." The fellow laughed. "Where's Sugar Kane now?" With a creak, the door shut.

I wormed out from under the cot. Six stayed on her belly. Days-old blood and vomit crusted her clothes.

Mine were no sweeter, with their layers of all-over-grease coated in coal dust, and my hands, too. All those miles of tunnel and no promising grate but this made me a specter not even a mother would welcome.

At the sight of me, Six pressed her spine to the wall, knees forming a barrier, the whites of her eyes enormous. Her pupils darted.

"Easy now." I offered the flat of my hands as if to a dog and sat on the end of the cot. "I'll not hurt you; I promise." That promise I intended to keep, like so many good intentions, was destined for the road to hell.

"Who…" The word all breath. Trying again, "…ou …e…" Her cheeks constricted.

I knew the gag, the metal that bit the tenderest bud and bone meant only for talk and the savoring of food. I knew the ache of knotted tendons, the pain of a shredded tongue, her gouged palate, the need to keep torn lips still.

Like twins, we two sat in this cell beset by a schism of mind. My body having lived what she lived. Unconscionable. Beyond reason. Indigestible.

I moved closer and touched her ankle. She grabbed my shirtfront, pointed at the door, then drew a finger across her throat.

"You'll get me killed?" My guess.

She nodded, the nod making her cough. Blood spattered my cheek.

I could feel again the tears, tongue minced, the blood I couldn't spit slipping into my throat. One blessing this time— they'd left her painless between the legs. Saved by a rogue stain, fear of new life holding her guards at bay.

"You want me gone?" I asked and prayed that she wouldn't, as I needed her. Together, we might escape. Until then, I'd be company, as she'd be to me. Another blessing I could count.

After my days crawling tunnels, thirst inhabited every organ. I had to have water. I scooped from her bucket, gave her a sip and drained the cup. "More," I encouraged her. Her swallow agonized both of us, but I had to have water. The bucket made no dent in my need, though I drank it just short of dry. "Should I leave?"

A twitch of her head said no, and I eased beside her. Like a blind man she ran fingers across my forehead, the bridge of my nose, over my cheeks with their warp of furnace burnt skin, along the tears at the corners of my mouth, scars the same as would be hers when the wounds healed. Her palms dragged across the prickles of my close-cropped hair, my bodily hunger draped in loose clothes, the weave and weft a match to hers.

We were like twins, both of us stringy, a sun-starved pallor stretched over bone. My body ached with the memory she worked to expunge.

All ridge and hollow, she folded her arms around me, rough shirt to rough shirt, breath to breath, the desperate touch, fingers again on my neck, chin, along my jaw, over a mole on my ear, not quite believing as I could not: this other, this being, this human, this person beside me.

Solitary no more. Dear, dear God. And with relief came the fear I'd be caught and cauterized in some unspeakable fashion.

She shivered in my arms. "Come," I said, "I'll cover you." Lifting her enough to pull off the blanket, I slipped behind her, spooned my warmth to her back, and pulled the blanket over us both.

Hours, maybe days, we stayed mostly on the mattress. Eventually the food slot sounded, but no food in evidence. Instead, a warning came—"Your choice, mad chair or mailman."

Six recognized the high voice, the chirpy laugh, Rat-Face detailing persuasions to come. "For your comfort, its padded." He gave a little snort.

I knew the chair in intimate detail. Six only knew the kind of chair. Sam had taken Chesterton to his barber, where seated and relaxed, the man swathed him in a sheet, shoulders to knees. The cloth caught hair as the barber trimmed his curls into submission, then took a stropped razor to his face. The sheet whisked away; he came out transformed. That's what his sister had claimed. That's what I knew firsthand.

Transformed: the results the Quakers wanted from Six. Silence: the scissors of their craft. Her guards had already violated the founders' code: speak only when necessary. This was the least of their violations.

Snickering came from the other side of the slot—more men joining Rat-Face as he continued his litany, "I'll strap you down, tie you like the wife's roast, only tighter. Much tighter."

Another's voice, "And no food in the mad chair. No water. Your nose'll itch," The very suggestion made Six scratch.

"Oh, leave her be," said blessed Ned, putting himself at risk. What would she do without Ned? Yet his kindness weakened her, made her want to cry.

The litany continued, "She's gotta know how fingers and toes'll tingle. Mmm. How many days, you ask."

She didn't ask. She didn't want to know. Not any of it.

"One day. Two? Maybe more, we'll see how you swell. Same as a roast, done when your skin turns black."

She shrank into the corner furthest from the slot. I perched on the table, fingering the Bible. "He's trying to scare you," I mouthed. "Don't listen."

"Yeah, Fergus knows tied," said another. "Like the wife ties his balls." More laughter, for once not at Six.

"Ball buster, ain't she? Not top dog here, not at home either." A crash of chains. Someone screamed.

"I'll do you, same as Six," Rat-Face was all-out of funning.

"No exaggeration," Ned whispered through the slot with dinner that night. "Just be good." He spoke the truth. My skin still harbored the mottle. But good meant giving his name. They'd put *him* in the mad chair. For starters.

Six shared her dinner that night and for many to follow. We made the best of her one wooden spoon.

When alone, she'd focused on the sick smell of mush and its accompaniments, but together, we went to Mamma's kitchen and laid a fire under the cauldron, her job after Father's accident. While the flames settled, we went to the henhouse. She selected the oldest hen, and with a quick twist dispatched the head.

Headless, the hen gyrated around the yard. Chickens will do that, but Sam had never thought to ask why. They just did. The running dead.

With practiced fingers she stripped feathers and down, all saved for bedding, then pinched the pinfeathers. With a sharp knife, she opened the bird's cavity. Steaming organs spilled. Entrails went to the pigs. Heart, liver, and gizzard saved for the fry pan. Head in the cauldron—the makings for soup along with gnawed bones.

At meals, we traded our favorite dishes; she, addicted to chicken parts breaded and fried; I preferred the bird whole, crisped over the coals, and both of us groaned with delight spooning in stew with biscuits and thick gravy. Though our stomachs filled with the unidentifiable, we tasted the past, spoonful by savory spoonful.

For days we stayed on her farm until I knew her mind as I know my own, forged in a communion of souls, our combined mettle sustaining us.

I hoped for continuous blessings similar to our dinners, but her old, darkening, days encroached.

℘☙☞

Outside the stable, Sam leaned on the paddock rail, overseeing Anna as she lunged Caesar. They hadn't had time for a ride. Lunging would have to do for the day's exercise.

Anna, in a full-length frock, braids a crown wound on her head, stood in the middle of the paddock, a firm grip on the thirty-foot strap attached to the horse's halter as he trotted a circle around her.

"Good," Sam called. "Now canter." She kept the light strap taught and clicked her tongue. "Canter," she commanded, her tone energetic. Caesar trotted faster.

"Need the whip?" Sam teased. The braided leather hung on the rail near Sam's elbow.

Anna scowled. "Hup, boy," she said, the command more energetic, and Caesar broke into a canter. Of course she wouldn't consider a whip. When riding, she refused spurs as well. She'd never used a crop.

Sam didn't like the whip either, and only carried it at Chesterton's request when working with Lucifer, as she had earlier in the day. Even with Lucifer, she never so much as flicked it.

From the lane, a rider advanced around the curve. "Anna," Barth called. "You're late. Tea's getting cold."

"I'm not finished," she called back.

He ignored Sam and slid off his horse before looping the reins over a post. "You'll be all day at this rate." With an elbow, he nudged Sam out of the way and vaulted into the paddock, lifting the whip as he went. "He's lazy." Barth pulled the lunge line from Anna's hand and popped the lash at Caesar. Eyes white-rimmed and rolling, the horse leapt to a gallop, the line vibrating.

"No!" Anna grabbed for the whip. "Stop it!"

Pulled one way by the lash, the other by the lunge line, Barth tipped on one leg. Anna let go and he fell, the leather strap snaking free in the dirt.

Sam slipped quietly through the gate and caught the line. "Steady now." Tone low, she reeled in the line and eased Caesar to smaller and smaller circles as he slowed to a standstill. "Atta boy." Sam patted his neck.

Trying not to seethe, she headed for the gate and passed Barth now sitting on the ground, the whip in the dirt at his side. She leaned and retrieved it, but as she straightened, he slammed his hand on the lash and yanked, pulling Sam off stride. Another yank brought her face down on top of him.

"What the hell?" he yelled. "Get offa me," and rolled on top of her. He gripped her wrists, holding them above her head, his chest flattened on hers. Belly to belly, his sheer mass overwhelmed her slighter body. Suffocated, she squirmed. Her legs in a scrabbling fury found no purchase.

"Not much of a fighter." Barth laughed.

"You brute." Anna stamped her boot. "Enough. Caesar needs a cool-down. You too. She pushed Barth's head.

"Move." He didn't. Her boot to his shoulder, she shoved him sideways. "Now."

Barth gave Sam a final grind into the dirt before he stood, straddling her hips. Disdainful, he loomed above her, and then stepped aside and brushed off his jodhpurs.

Spit or scream, Sam couldn't decide which—take a breath Sam. "I'll…" her voice ragged, "…walk Caesar." She hoped the paddock dust would cover her fury. Or was it humiliation?

To think there'd been a time she found him enticing, even…. Her gorge rose. She had to bury that. Purge herself of any lingering delusion.

Anna marched for the stable, whip and lunge line in hand, while Barth mounted his horse and cantered in the opposite direction. Sam, still seething, took Caesar to the back forty.

⁪⁫

Six balled her fists. "I've got to be good, got to be."

Good, be good, a mantra, repeated ad nauseam along with every little detail set to rights—the Bible, on top of the extra handkerchief, had to be square to the table corner; the handkerchief squared to the Bible; her wood spoon licked clean, rinsed, and placed parallel beside the Bible's spine; the extra socks paired, folded, and set perpendicular to the table's wall-side; and God forbid if the alignments varied by a quarter of a thumbnail.

In the cold we shared the bed, generous on her part, my knees tucked behind hers, her back to my front. Though spooned warmth worked for us both, the small rocks she had collected and laid in a line under the blanket at our feet were not workable. Their marks dotted our ankles blue and black. She didn't care. I did.

Her calves cramped in the night and I stayed wakeful, thinking about how Mamma used to heat rounded stones in the fire, wrap them in a towel, and for hours keep everyone's feet warm. Here, the blanket had to suffice and would, Six insisted, if placed over her shoulder, below her chin, tucked under curled legs, and in the morning, body heat remained, and we made it into the bed. The blanket must be smooth on top, with the edge a finger's length off the floor, which she scrubbed with precious drinking water.

"Please, blanket to the floor," I begged her. "They'll see me. Is that what you want?"

She frowned, fists at her mouth, wheels turning. She wouldn't sell me out for a few inches of uneven blanket. Or would she?

The time I kicked the table leg, knocking everything an inch out of whack, I learned not to tease. She shoved me, two-handed and hard. She said in my ear, "They'll get me, they will, you don't understand, you don't know what they're like, they see through walls, they'll know, and it's the mad chair. Be good, I've got to be. Got to."

"What good has *good* done you? Look at yourself." But she wouldn't. She squinched her eyes like the light was too bright. "Be a worm, and that's how they treat you." I pushed her. "Stand up."

"No, no, no." She folded her arms over her head and scuttled in circles as if I'd struck her, as if I chased her to strike again. Sometimes I wanted to, but it wouldn't help us escape. She needed calm, and I lured her back to the farm, to what should have been quieter days.

∞℘

Sam cooled Caesar and herself with the help of clouds across the late-day sun. She took in the scent of mums, deep red and bedded by the shortcut Anna probably took. Too late for tea, no doubt.

Sam had feeding and watering yet to do and looked forward to an evening ride exercising Lucifer in relative peace. Caesar on the lead, she approached the stable, and the breeze carried a contentious jabber. Indistinct, sharp edges getting sharper. Rounding the corner, closer to the main door, she heard argument, the parties easily identified.

Barth should've been home. Anna too, explaining her absence to Auntie. They should never have been alone together.

"I said no," Anna, peevish. "I've told you before, I won't keep company, not with you, not tonight, not next week, not next month. No! How many times…"

"What, I'm not good enough?" Barth, volume rising, "You prefer an ignorant stable hand?"

"So ignorant—Sam's going to university. And you? What's schooling done for you? If your father…"

Sam left Caesar in the paddock, his stall still needing attention. She stood to the side of the open door, lead line in hand. Despite work to do, she didn't want to intrude on this well-deserved dressing-down.

"Professor be damned, my father runs the county," Barth said. "Think, your family and mine allied, we'd rule. Hell, we could rule the country. It's the smart move."

"You… You want Meadowvale!" A moment of silence. It broke with a hiss. "Sssso, Papa wouldn't sell. And this way…" she shouted, "…it's free."

Horses shifted in their stalls. One nickered. Another stamped. "If you were the last man on earth, I wouldn't marry you."

A scuffle, boots on cobbles, on straw. Sam peeked around the doorframe. The aisle between the stalls stood empty, Caesar's stall door ajar. With the resounding clang of a bucket, water flowed out.

Anna, her words a fist, "…nothing but spoiled. A little boy, that's what you are." Feet scrambled.

"Little boy, am I!" Something tore.

Sam bolted for the stall. All she could see through partition bars were their heads as they struggled. Barth's yellow hair ragged. Anna's braids, loose from their crown, flailed across her face as she wrenched at his grip.

"I'll..." Barth low and savage. "Show *you...*"

"No!" She shrieked. "Nooo..."

Sam flung the door wide. Lurching into the dim box, she tripped on the empty bucket. With a clang, it took her down, all fours hard on a skim of kicked-about straw.

The moon of Barth's naked rump glowed white in a corner of the stall. Jodhpurs around his knees, he pressed a forearm across Anna's pale breasts, shoving her against the haymow. The other hand grappled underneath her skirts.

"Barth." Sam tripped to her feet. "For God-sake, stop!"

He turned, face mottled, lips twisted. "I don't take orders from servants."

She was too slight compared to Barth. How could Sam stop him? She needed a weapon. With none to hand, she hooked the handle of the bucket, and in two strides, swung it. The metal rim grazed his shoulder. He lashed a fist at her face, but his pants caught at the top of his spurred boots and hobbled him.

The swing wild, he hit Sam's ear, a glancing blow, and went down. "You son of a..." On his knees, he hauled at his pants, and one boot under him, lunged. Sam didn't wait for both boots to launch his full weight, and using the bucket as a battering ram, she knocked him flat.

On him in a second, she planted her knees on his broad chest. The bucket held high, she fought herself as she would another person, wanting to bash him until he bled. Bash him until he broke. God, how she wanted to blind him with his own blood. He deserved worse.

Her arms shook. Barth, lips aquiver, cowered beneath her. Sam had never been so tempted.

"Justice is Mine, sayeth the Lord." It wasn't her place to mete it out. That was when the seep of blood appeared, a growing circle on his white shirt visible through a tear in his jacket. Anna's screams pierced Sam's rage, "...pleeeease stop!" Tears streamed down her cheeks.

Shame wheeled her. "Oh, Anna." Sam stripped her jacket and, rushing to Anna, slipped it on and closed it over the torn frock.

Anna's words came in hiccups, "He...he would..."

From the stall door, Barth sneered. "This isn't over."

"Get out," Sam snarled, lips tight to her teeth.

Barth buttoned his jodhpurs. "I promise, you'll pay." He cinched his belt tight and wincing, shook his fist as he left the stable.

An arm around Anna's shoulder, Sam gently pulled her toward the stall door. "Sam, your ear," she said. "It's bleeding."

In her rage she hadn't felt it, but now, the sting came through. Sam touched the ridge. Her fingers came away red.

"Give me your handkerchief." Anna took it and staunched the seep. She opened her hand. "Oooh, the mole, it's torn." She dabbed the blood from Sam's cheek.

"Anna, enough, it's fine," she said. "Come, we'll find your father."

Anna halted. "We can't." She turned, a tight hold on Sam's arm. "No one must know."

"You'd say nothing after he t-touched you?"

She shook her head, two vehement twitches. "He's right. I would pay."

"Surely he meant me." Sam put her hand over Anna's.

Anna pulled away to the middle of the stall. "I'd be shamed; me and my family, shamed before everyone. It would kill Auntie." She retreated against the stall partition. "God knows what Papa might do. And Barth didn't actually... Either way, he'd deny it."

"I saw him. He *would* have..." Sam blanched at the thought.

"Look at what happened to your father," she said. "Besides, no one would believe you over Kane's son." Anna slumped against the wall.

"But surely, they'd believe *you*." Sam held her hands.

"No, promise me, Sam. Promise you'll say nothing."

CHAPTER 47

ARRESTED

The days had stayed warm, though red leaves hinted at changes to come, warmth allowing for a last slap at slow-moving mosquitoes. Pumpkins swelled in the garden beside crook-necked squash, their vines invading domains of late lettuce, now bolted and left too bitter to eat.

And beside them, the asparagus patch ferned out with fronds spread high as Sam's chest, rich with the promise of a hearty crop next spring. Red berries speckled feathery greens, giving another vision of plenty.

A trove of carrots, saved for fresh picking until well after frost, waited underground, along with beets, parsnips, and turnips. Mamma and Sam, bending double, had already picked the greener fare. They'd pickled and jarred and stored all of it on shelves in the earthen cellar, sustenance against the long months ahead.

At dinner, Mamma said, "Your ear's healing well. So, what did happen?"

Sam touched the ridge of her ear. It was still tender.

She'd hardly felt the strike of Barth's ring, and now, her mind consumed with his threat, his voice echoed as loud as a fire bell. It took Sam's attention from the spread before her. Her mother's efforts languished on the plate: lamb chops, baked squash with fresh churned butter, broccoli, sweet potato, and on the windowsill, an apple pie cooled.

Sworn to silence, what could Sam say? What would Barth say? Surely, humiliation would silence him too.

Yet the echo continued, and over it came the sound of a knock at the front door.

Mamma looked up with a start. Father laid his fork and knife on the edge of his plate, and aided by a cane, pushed up from his chair. The knock pounded.

"Coming," he called, his limp hurried. But short of the door, it burst open.

Two constables strode in. "Sam Lawson, come with us." They advanced on the table. Before she could rise, they each took an arm and pulled her to her feet.

"What is this?" Father thumped his cane on the floor.

"An arrest."

"Can't Sam finish dinner?" Mamma asked, bewildered tears brimming.

"Mayhem with intent," one said. Behind Sam's back, they wound a rope around her wrists. "No dinner."

"Sam?" Father wobbled and leaned two-handed on his cane. "What...?"

"An altercation with Barth," she said.

"Altercation, my arse." The constables pushed her to the door. "The Kane boy, his arm's useless."

Hustled out of the cottage, Sam looked back over her shoulder. "That's not..."

Mamma held to Father, who held to his cane. Incredulous eyes wide, they stood on the threshold. Sam wanted to say more, so many things, but there was no time before they put her in their cart and rattled down the lane.

Yet, had there been time, she couldn't have said more. She'd promised, and she wouldn't so much as hint at what Barth had done.

And she wouldn't lie. As a Quaker, she couldn't.

Yet, without truth, what defense could there be?

CHAPTER 48

LOCKUP

If it hadn't been for Anna's Auntie, Sam knew Anna would sing sweet as the evening peepers. Instead, truth sat on her tongue—a green frog silent and sweating.

In lockup, as things grew ugly, Sam got the story in depth. It passed from the scullery maid who Chesterton had to let go, to her cousin making beds at the inn by the canal, to the barkeep who slept with the girl who Kane slept with too, to the girl who swept Sam's cell—mum's the word, the official one, but bets, with money attached, kept speculation infectious.

"Young Kane's the one done sung," a cellmate said. Sam couldn't believe Barth would tell all, and hearing more, it sounded like a chorus in harmony with his father, the boy parroting the man: an expanded fancy in differing shades of detail no one dared question. When Mrs. Kane had been interviewed, Mr. Kane said, "Mrs. Kane has no opinion." He had enough opinions for them both but played it close. All would be revealed when the circuit judge came in six or eight months.

"Justice can't wait," so said the prosecutor. "This case needs to be heard while the facts are fresh." Through an undisclosed process, a Philadelphia judge had been found and pressed into service. Truth would out.

CHAPTER 49

TRIAL

Before the judge came, Sam languished for three weeks in the town's makeshift lockup. The bare room behind the constable's office had benches against the walls and a high window set with bars. Mamma brought two meals a day, there being no provision for long incarceration, such as a bed, and no way to accommodate visitors, even though Mamma waited to take back the dirty dishes.

For those weeks, especially on weekends, Sam fidgeted in company with serial drunks, brawlers, petty thieves, and escaped slaves, all men who passed through quickly without aid of the extended system of justice. The Philadelphia judge—a Court Jester, one wag called him—had a habit of pulling facts from a hat in a rabbit-like fashion. The wag's comment held no traction after his release. Nothing believable in the word of one more drunk.

Sam pled guilty, eager to get through the proceedings, serve her time, and get home. Waiting had her chewing the inside of her cheek.

She *had* struck Barth, and besides, her family couldn't afford a lawyer. With no contest, the formalities would be over in a matter of minutes, court consisting of a hearing before the judge pronounced sentence. She'd be sent to Cherry Hill. Not Auburn, thank God.

Her court date came, and the constable brought her to his office where Mamma, holding Father's arm, waited. She'd aged in three weeks, her eyes red above cheeks gray as her frock, brown pillows under her eyes. She broke from Father and took Sam in her arms. Pressed her close. Silent weeping shook them both.

Father stood stiff as if winter had eclipsed the fall and congealed him. With a few minutes to thaw, he rested a hand on

Sam's back. "Paul wanted to come," he said. "We told him no, nothing to be done, best stay at his studies." Father patted her shoulder. "Soon, you'll be released." His attempt at a smile was so bleak, she couldn't look. "Paul will bring you home."

"Time's a-wasting," the constable said. "Your mamma brought clean clothes." He indicated the table with a metal bowl next to a change of pants and shirt. "You can wash your face." No washcloth, no towel in evidence, no soap, just a small puddle of water in the bowl.

Sam closed her eyes and splashed her face, scrubbing with the flat of her hands. The wet she drew down her jaw and around her neck felt wonderful. Unbraiding her hair, she combed it with her fingers. Re-plaited, the braid hung on her back.

At the roots, a crawling sensation remained as the constable took her to the outhouse to change her clothes. Poor Mamma, no dress the right size—she must have hated bringing the usual pants and shirt. Just as well. In lockup she was safer as a boy.

Sam entered the courtroom with a constable on either side. She frowned. Confusion gripped her as she took in the roomful of people. The gallery was packed. At the far end of the room an empty desk stood on a cobbled-together platform, to the right a section with twelve chairs, twelve men seated.

The constables guided her down the aisle between onlookers, to a table facing the high desk. Sam took a seat, the constables beside her.

Behind them in the gallery Mamma sat, her face grayer yet. Her chin quivered. Beside her, Father sat rigid. He stared at his fingers locked unmoving in his lap. No doubt this was an attempt to avoid the eyes of Kane and his wife. They sat with Barth in the front row, their breath on the neck of a man, most likely the prosecutor, sitting at a table similar to Sam's.

"All rise."

The judge in full robes entered from behind the high desk. He climbed the platform. He sat. The gavel banged.

"Hear ye, hear ye," the bailiff called. "As the charges against the defendant, Samuel Lawson, have been raised from mayhem to attempted homicide, the case before Judge Horace Purdy this day will be heard by a jury. Please be seated."

"How do you plead?" the judge asked.

Sam gave her father a frantic glance. "Homicide?" She looked back at the Judge. "I didn't intend..."

"Not guilty." The judge banged his gavel.

Sam sat forward in her seat. "I meant..."

"Not now," he said. "When you testify. Under oath."

Her hand on the Bible, she promised to tell the truth, and nothing but. This wasn't supposed to happen. She'd worked out the truth she could tell and not compromise Anna.

Now, how could Sam keep her promise to God and Anna at the same time? Anna and Sam, their bond a mutual understanding forged further in the heat of this hidden confidence, their lives now caught in a twisted imbalance.

Silence. Only silence could save Anna.

CHAPTER 50

WINTER WASHING

In prison, only holding her tongue could save Ned.

As a cold breeze blew under Six's sliding door, she set the water bucket on the table, centered it at the near edge, dipped cupped hands, and splashed her face. With her fingers she scrubbed the crevices behind her ears.

"I shouldn't have to remind you," I said. "We drink that water."

"Yes, clean." Hands rinsed, she dried herself with the tail of her jacket. "Nearly there." She hitched her shoulders as if a spider crawled under her collar. Off came her jacket and shirt. She dipped the shirt in the bucket, wrung it, and scrubbed. She scrubbed again at her cheeks and down the cords of her neck.

"Don't," I said, "It's all we have." A hands-width of water at the bottom of the bucket, and it was cloudy enough already. Another method Rat-Face used to subdue her after the warden turned watchful. Or so said the priest, who piled on God's guilt.

She paid no attention to him or me and rubbed the shirt over her breastbone. She scrubbed around depleted hillocks, down the hollow of her belly, and twisting the shirt to a thick rope, tossed it over one shoulder, sawing across her back. "Godliness, yes," she said.

"Enough!" I hissed, afraid she'd take off her pants and socks and wash them too. She'd freeze if she did, with nothing dry to change into. She scowled as she wrung the last drops into the bucket. Unwinding the rope, she flapped it. She slipped her arms into the sleeves and buttoned the jacket on top.

The very thought of her wet shirt gave me the shivers.

Bucket back under the table and centered at the wall side, she wiped at drips, floor and table, with her sleeve. She dusted the Bible and set the spoon in line with its spine.

Under the table, she, on hands and knees, realigned the growing number of rocks.

Patted them into place out of view against the wall.

Annoyed, though I knew better, I kicked the table leg. Her carefully positioned collection barely moved.

In a rage, she flew at me. Her unclipped fingernails raked my jacket. Her fists battered my chest.

I grabbed her wrists. "Resorting to violence?" As quickly as she flared, she crumpled on the cot and stared at the stone ceiling.

Crazed patterns lined the whitewash above her. Some sections curled off the stone, the black underside of the paint exposed. She wanted to peel it, the way that, after a long harvest, she'd peel strips of sunburn off her arms, a compulsion she couldn't stop until she'd stripped dead skin down to living flesh.

A spider picked its way along the cracks, dropped, and swung on a thread, caught silver as it crossed the skylight shaft. At home, before screens, the family relied on spiders to rid the house of mosquitoes. The plump blood-suckers blundered into the snare, and by morning they'd be wrapped and hung from the web, gone golden with sun streaming through her bedroom window.

In the house, she'd blessed the spider and hurried off to continue her day. In her cell, watching the spider pounce on a frantic mosquito, bite it, and wrap it, the strands drawn tighter and tighter, made her hurt. And she hurt more when the spider ate it, starting with its prey's delicate legs, as if starting with her own fingers and moving on... She closed her eyes and the trial came back.

8003

"Samuel Lawson." the prosecutor stood at his table. "Did you on June third, in the stable of your employer, Ryan Chesterton, strike Bartholomew Kane causing grievous bodily harm?"

"Sam-mule" is what she heard, though there was no Paul there to laugh at this joke. Without pause she answered, "I swung a bucket. *By accident*, it tore his jacket and shirt." She rested her hands on her thighs, stiff fingers out straight.

"And he bled." The man came from behind his table. "Isn't that so?"

"Yes, I made him bleed, a happening I profoundly regret." This was no lie; she did regret her failure of conscience, and she regretted the continuing satisfaction she felt in the pain she'd inflicted, though she suspected a spot of malingering under the sling Barth wore into court.

"Regret because you're now in court charged with attempted murder?"

"No, sir." Her fingers curled. "Because striking anyone goes against my beliefs. I would never attempt to kill."

"And the reason for this so-called accident?" He raised an eyebrow.

"Barth was trespassing. I asked him to stop."

"In fact, he had escorted his mother who came by invitation to tea with Miss Chesterton, and on his way home he stopped to assist with an unruly horse. Isn't that the case? And you attacked him in the paddock as well." He pointed at her. "In fact, you had long-standing feelings against him stemming from your infatuation..." He turned to the jury with a smug smile. "...with the younger Miss Chesterton."

Infatuation? Long-standing feelings against him, yes, in a myriad ways, though none stemming from infatuation with Anna. To claim innocence would only raise more skepticism from the judge and the mumbling rabble in the gallery.

Sam's protective instincts flared. A flush pricked her neck. It rose to her cheeks as the rabble's interpretation dug below decency.

She hated their intense interest at every mention of Anna's name. The grizzled men tasted it, passed it back and forth, clothes falling, her image enflamed in their eyes.

For all Sam's silence, carnal implications floated in the room. Try as she might to quell them, she kept making things worse. Her fingers dug into her thighs.

Sam had to calm herself. She took a slow breath. "The stable is beyond the house—not on young Kane's way home. And he hadn't been invited by Ann...Miss Chesterton or me to be at the stable." Her words coming faster, "He certainly hadn't been invited to use a whip..." She forced her fingers flat on her thighs. "...a whip on a horse that answered to voice command."

"Young Mr. Kane simply wanted to help," the judge interrupted. "He testified that you stood outside the paddock and leaned on the fence, doing nothing."

"I'd been teaching Miss Chesterton the proper tone to..."

"And what about *your* tone? Do you always command your betters to do your bidding?"

The prosecutor crossed his arms over his chest, and waited as the judge went on: "Do you always snatch things, if your betters don't obey? And, as you did later in the stable, bludgeon someone in retribution for ignoring you?"

So much truth here, when couched in this fashion. Sam wanted to defend herself, *Is young Kane a better trainer than I?*

Chesterton, in his testimony, had made Sam's stellar talents clear, how trusted she was, her decorum with Anna, all the extra time she took in Anna's education. Again, the knowing snickers had come from the gallery.

"In this case," Sam kept her voice low and humble and told the absolute truth, "My first responsibility was to Mr. Chesterton's horses, maintaining their safety and his daughter's as she learned how a stable operates. This meant clearing the premises of distractions."

"You mean young Kane?" The prosecutor said.

"Yes. He made it clear he didn't intend to leave. The horse having been whipped; I couldn't return it to the stall with him in the way."

"Miss Anna was there in the stable?"

"Yes, she brushes the horse after each training. She was late for tea, and I had more chores to finish. I didn't know what else to do."

Several members of the jury turned to each other. Some nodded, seeming to understand Sam's quandary, and cast sympathetic glances her way. Enough people had seen Barth hunting to know the kind of a horseman he was, and they cared about their horses the way Chesterton did. It seemed like Sam had a chance at simple assault. Hope kindled in her chest.

Kane rushed forward from the gallery, his brows clamped. A muscle jumped in his cheek. He beckoned to the prosecutor and bent to his ear in animated whisperings.

The man turned an eye to Barth and back to the judge, saying, "Your honor, a moment, please."

"You're excused," the judge said, and Sam returned to her table.

The courtroom went silent as Kane motioned Barth to the table. They sat on either side of the prosecutor, their heads together, voices too low to hear words. Their angry faces blared a clear message. Minutes passed.

"Mr. Kane?" said the judge. The whispering continued. "Enough now."

The prosecutor stood. "I call Bartholomew Kane to the stand."

Barth, immaculate with clean yellow hair trimmed at the ears, his shirt crisp and white, a yellow vest the only suggestion of color under his dark brown frock coat, walked to the witness chair. One arm in a black sling, he awkwardly flipped his coattail and sat at attention.

"Do you swear to tell the truth and nothing but, so help you God?"

"I do," Barth said, his eyes round with innocence.

"Please," said the prosecutor, "tell the court what you just told me."

"I didn't want to bring this up. I know how much reputation means to Anna and her family. I wanted to protect her. That's why I wouldn't leave the stall. The defendant...," everyone called Sam that, as if she wasn't a person. Barth pointed a shaky finger at Sam, "He raped her."

"Rape" hung in the air a split second before pandemonium struck.

CHAPTER 51

TRIAL

Rape. Gasps exploded, followed by shouted chatter. The judge banged his gavel. "Order. Order."

Father surged from his seat. "He lies." He gave a mirthless laugh and marched out of the gallery toward the witness chair. "Sam isn't…"

"Bailiff." The judge hammered his desk.

Father stood with his hand high, a professor making his point. "I'll prove…"

"Bailiff, evict this man."

"No, listen, she's…"

"OUT!"

With the bailiff busy evicting Father, Sam stood, "But, sir…" The constables pulled her into her chair.

"Not another word." He slammed his gavel. "Young Kane, you may continue."

"I saw him leave the horse in the paddock and return to the stable. I knew Anna had been waiting inside to finish the brushing. She'd never leave a job half done, even though she'd already missed tea with my mother and her aunt. I knew Sam wouldn't help her, too important, too busy. I'd offer to help.

"I thought it strange when he left the horse outside; wasn't sure what to do, hurry things and bring the horse in? He made me nervous, being so angry before he cooled Caesar."

Glued in disbelief, Sam sat forward in her chair, fingers dug into her knees.

"I wish I hadn't waited. If only I'd gone in sooner, I could have stopped…."

A commotion in the gallery broke the testimony as Chesterton tried to hustle his sister and daughter from the room. Anna wouldn't budge, her white lips compressed. The elder Miss

Chesterton flowed through the courtroom door as if carried on a puff of rarified air. Unable to get Anna quietly out, Chesterton nudged her into the row two behind Sam.

Barth sighed. His head drooped, though not far enough to hide wistful eyes from the jury. "By that time, I was truly worried, and then she screamed. I ran in, and there he was in the stall on top of her. She batted his face and yelled, "Stop. Stop.""

"I shouted at him. Caught in the act, he jumped off her, grabbed the water bucket, and swung it. Lucky it wasn't full; he'd have killed me then and there, and who knows what he'd have done to Anna.

"The bucket caught my shoulder, wounding me so I couldn't use my arm." Palm up toward the bad arm in its sling, he tapped it and winced. "Anna ran out. I figured she'd be safe, go to her parents. I guess she didn't, too embarrassed. Or maybe they told her if anyone discovered a servant had raped her, her chances at marriage…. Well, this injustice bothered me."

"You know," the judge said, "you're ruining her chance at marriage now. Your testimony could ruin her life. Yet here you are?"

"I have to. I couldn't let him…."

"A fine sentiment, but we'll need corroboration. I'm sure you understand. I call young Miss Chesterton."

Sam eased back in her chair. At least she would be exonerated. But Anna. What of Anna?

CHAPTER 52

INFRACTION

Frozen puddles stomped to a tantrum of cracks

Rape—the word slammed Six afresh as if Barth had just said it. We sat on the cot, my arm over her shoulder, and I pulled her close.

Cold engulfed the cell. "How could he…." She flung free of my arm. Paced, door to slot and back. "I wish I'd killed….." She stopped, head tipped back, fists digging into her eyes. "No. No, never."

She fell to her knees on the floor and slammed the cot with her fists, twisted and wound the blanket around her head. Stuffed a fold in her mouth. The wool rasped wounds on her tongue as the blanket absorbed spit. Self-hooded, she screamed into the muffling wool.

Finally exhausted, she crawled onto the cot, the blanket falling around her shoulders. I sat at her side and rubbed her feet.

With a clack, the food slot opened. The usual aroma of something questionable worked its way through the cell. Could she taste a vegetable if properly cooked, or that mess purporting to be meat?

The smell rekindled her fury. "Pork," she snarled out loud, not that she'd smelled it.

"Watch yourself," I whispered.

"They have pork," she said, full volume.

I, too, had seen the scalding tank, the pulleys.

"Who gets the pork?" she demanded, and rushed the slot, her blanket abandoned on the floor. "Not me, I don't get pork." Hands on the metal, she pressed her face in the opening. "Hey, Rat-Face! Do you get ham?"

"Don't!" I kept my voice low. "Remember the mad chair." She'd seen my blackened toes.

"Warden!" she shrieked, and wouldn't stop. "Do *you* get ribs? *Do* you?"

A key grated in the lock. I grabbed the blanket, threw myself left of the door, and fell in the corner. Balled under cover, I hoped I made a convincing pile of nothing unusual. I counted on people seeing what they expected to see. They'd focus on the task at hand, their eyes rarely straying to what they'd assume were empty spaces.

And then I prayed. I prayed Six wouldn't look my way. If she did, the guard would know, and only God knew what would happen then.

CHAPTER 53

COUNTING BLESSINGS

*A hog is a hog
except when it's Six*

They, Rat-Face, Bigger, Tall-Boy, left the doors open. I heard her fury lashing the three of them out through the yard and down the alley. My back to the wall, I followed.

She'd been ushered into the tub room before, allowed an occasional bath. This time, they dragged her into the lamplight. No hood. They slammed the door, but too hard and the latch bounced. The door ajar, I watched from the hall as they flung her to the floor and stripped her the way they had that first day. She drew knees to elbows, eyes clamped, and crossed her ankles. One hand shifted between her legs. No rogue stain.

The many-fingered air made free with her, sliding against her thighs and rump, touching, touching. She curled tight as a salted slug.

Salted, the slug would exude an ocean of water, and truly mortify. Not so for her. Though her cheeks went wet and salty, Death took no notice.

Having shared past dreams, our hopes and happenings, I could feel every breath, feel every finger touching her, as they'd touched me, making me think her thoughts before she did. So many places she couldn't cover, I knew she wished she had a tail to tuck between her legs. And before a hand could caress where no hand but hers had touched, a veil blotted the unholy unfoldings.

My body knew how hands would roll her, belly to the cold stone, and tie her hands behind her back, a position not conducive to bathing. How she'd find herself lying at the base of the tank. Knew her curled spine, knew the boot on each side of her rump pressing her flat, her legs nudged apart. A pole would be set from ankle to ankle. Six would be chained in place, the way Sam had chained a hog ready for scalding.

"Count yourself blessed," Rat-Face said. "Cold water."

"Yes, blessed," said the priest, who came from the shadows, Bible in his hand. "Blessed with so many chances." He made the sign of the cross. "If only you'd given a name." He moved closer. "I tried. I did my best, but you wouldn't repent." He opened the Bible and mumbled psalms in a wordless hum.

"You're out of chances," said Rat-Face.

From the door, I could hear him smile, hear him draw ropes through the pulleys, hear the clunk of a hook hitting the floor. He'd flip her face up to the room, arms crushed, and fasten the hook through the bar's central ring. He'd pull the rope taut, haul her up, feet first. She'd bend at the middle as her rump lifted, shoulders scraping the floor. Up, up, until toes at the ceiling, her body would swing free. And it did.

The motion brought nausea. She clenched her fists, long fingernails digging into her palms.

Sam's hog hadn't writhed before scalding. Of course, Six wasn't a hog. Her value was so much less against the ledgers of the day. She, merely female, was more akin to a worm skewered on a fishhook. No, not even that. Without children, more like chaff after harvest.

Count yourself fortunate. She'd grind her fingernails harder into her palms. Fortunate, she'd try anything to distract from the next minute and the minute after that, as Rat-Face lowered her head first into the water. "Your mailman, Wee-Ned, wasn't it? Say his name."

Inch by inch water seeped through her short hair. Hair was another identity, stolen along with her name. Count now. Count anything.

Happy happenstance: One: No heat off the water, its surface gray and still as an old bath. Quite so, take comfort—

Two: hooked to the rope. No barb ran belly to gullet as she'd done to worms time and again without thought when fishing for eel.

Three: Not dead. Not yet. A blessing?

Take comfort, this ducking so different from those ducked before her time. Before, a female would sit right-side up, tied in a chair on the end of a plank. The woman would be fully dressed in a long gray frock, looking like Mamma.

Oh, Mamma.

Often the woman was drowned by mistake, proving that she wasn't a witch.

Should the woman live—glory be, proof positive that she'd been a witch after all. In the face of such "undisputable truth," they'd set her on fire.

"Undisputable!" Father had raged, still incensed at injustices he thought, they'd all thought, had long since been abandoned.

Six felt the skin give beneath her nails. That pain was a blessing.

Four? Five? With drowning likely, she found it hard to count her comforts. She'd stick to numbers.

Count each stab of her nails—Nine, ten. Fear loosened Ned's name. Poor Ned.

The water rose through her hair and over her forehead. Twelve. It invaded her ears, her eyes. She squinched her nose.

Seventeen, eighteen… Swimming in the pond, she'd held her nose between thumb and forefinger to the count of ninety. Totally submerged in spring-fed water, she'd watched catfish, their long whiskers combing the bottom, their movements fluid. If only she could swim like that, clear eyes scanning for minnows, and hold her breath forever.

No minnows to scan, breath running out, so hard to count, and raised clear of the water, she gasped. A blessing she could count. One.

"Give us the name."

A blessing was Ned. She held his name the way she held her breath, its bursting insistence sharp in her chest. His name tripped on her tongue, staggered, as if the man himself danced to the tip.

Ned could spill, another second, would spill, but the rope dropped her again. Ned clamoring her pipes, she squeezed her fists harder. Fingernails dug into her palms. Self-inflicted, the pain diluted theirs, her flight of mind something the hog never needed to use.

Lucky hog, she'd been killed and bled before hoisting. She didn't have to see the anticipation as, with each pull, her body tipped. She didn't have to hear the squeak of stifled titillation when her nakedness swung over the tank.

Breath out, Ned slippery on Six's tongue. To tell would be a thousand deaths.

To die? Just one. A relief. She envied the hog. So many ways. She should count them.

Rising from the tank, the hog didn't blink away water. The hog didn't know the peering eyes.

Didn't know how pupils danced. How grins quivered on her tormentors' faces. How they took turns at the rope, dropping, lifting.

The hog didn't feel the creatures' pinch and prod in never-touched places as water slid into her windpipe. Didn't see the onlookers' near-shuddering pleasure.

The hog never knew the worst of what it was to be a woman.

CHAPTER 54

AFTER THE COUNT

"You want a turn, Father?" asked Rat-Face, his voice emanating from another world.

Their talk of no concern, she opened her mouth to say so. Nothing came out but bubbles. It all seemed moot. As she slipped toward black, her hands relaxed. Fingers uncurled, palms open, red holes on display.

"Stop," snapped the priest, his command sharp. "My God."

Rat-Face paused on the rope, Six's mouth just clear of the water. "No, we haven't a name." He let her sink.

"Now." The force of the priest's office was clear.

Rat-Face hoisted. Her body swung. She dripped.

The drips, increasingly red, ran rivulets down her arms, dropped off her shoulders, and spread in the gray water.

"Let her down." The priest grabbed the rope. It eased, and taking her weight, he lowered her gently past the metal lip to the floor. "Free her," he said, his watery eyes fastened on her hands. "She's redeemed."

"You old fool." Rat-Face laughed. "She did it herself. On purpose."

"And the scars at her mouth? Dark mottle on her skin? I could report those as well."

"Warden wants a name. We can't let it go."

"And the inspector?"

Rat-Face kicked the metal rod between her ankles. He leaned at Six's face. "I'll have you yet," he mouthed and turned his back, leaving the priest and Bigger to unchain her.

ൠ ൠ

I ran back to the cell and all the dim day agonized over her return. When they brought her in, they'd come completely into the cell. The guards would find me.

They'd be relaxed, observant. How could they miss me, with no need to fight her with every step? There'd be no fight left.

Under the bed, my toes could protrude. Knees could peek out the side.

Too bad I couldn't be a spider, crawl up the stones, and watch from on high. Or could I?

I leaned on the wall, hands flat, and stretched until my heels hit the opposite stones.

I flexed and lifted one foot to hip level. Heels pressed to uneven stone, I slid the opposite hand higher on the opposing wall. Tall of body, I bridged the cell.

A foot length at a time, alternating hands and feet, I hiked higher until the arch of my spine hit the vaulted ceiling, and below, the empty cell had the aspect of a dollhouse.

My muscles quivered. Alive with new excitement, I slid down.

When the time came, Rat-Face, Bigger, and Tall-Boy entering, the trick would be in the clockwork. I needed time to climb, but not so many minutes on high that my muscles would give, and I'd drop, more stone than spider, and like a stone, no thread to save me. If I fell, maybe I'd crush them.

Day passed into night. They wouldn't bring her back until morning, assuming they hadn't tied the ropes wrong when they hung her to dry.

She knew I'd be here waiting. I'd care for her, know the things she could never tell another, her private doubts and humiliations, and soothe them as another never could.

ဆာ

Morning came. I'd slept in her bed, taken the plate from the slot, but not eaten. She'd need it even if she couldn't stomach the thought.

I stretched the muscles of my arms and legs, bent forward, bent back, ran small steps, warming to the task ahead. Full light shone on me, such as it was through the skylight. I kept an ear cocked to the yard.

On returning, I'd left the doors open, same as the guards had, so I listened for the whisper of sock-covered boots. And there...

Feet and hands in position I spidered up, up, to the sound of boots scuffing the rubble. One set.

He wouldn't look up. No one would, and possibly being foolish, I counted on it.

Six's nakedness glared in Ned's arms as he laid her gently on the cot. The other guards' fun at an end, Ned had the task of hosing her free of secretions and excretions too noxious for the tender nostrils of Rat-Face and his closer companions. Her palms oozed. Ned covered her with the blanket.

My legs quivered. Too many minutes had passed. I wanted to reset my feet, but he'd hear me. Flaking whitewash would fall, and he'd be sure to look.

My arms got into the need, and the quiver turned tremble. Ned dropped her clothes on the table.

From the door he looked back over his shoulder to the cot and sighed. Sighed down to the toes of his sock-covered boots.

Go, go, go; I tried to move him with the power of will alone, and keep still myself. Not much longer, and I'd be that stone.

My weaker leg shook, the foot looser on the wall. I countered with the opposite hand, straining for pressure.

Don't. Don't let go.

He stepped over the sill, shook his head, and slowly slid the door closed. I fought the relief that would let me fall, and inch by shuddering inch, lowered myself. With three feet left, I crumpled to the floor in a bone-jarred heap.

It took minutes to be able to stand and force one foot in front of the other and over to the cot. I touched Six's cheek with trembling fingers.

She gasped. Her eyes sprang open as if she'd just surfaced. I could feel the cold-water burn radiant under her ribs, the red washed eyes, the gouged palms.

"Oh, Six." And I crawled under the blanket, held her, her skin against my coarse clothes, her breath ragged, both of us shivering.

CHAPTER 55

ANNA

"By request of the Chesterton family," said the judge, "young Miss Chesterton has not been called to testify, her health cited as precarious, but these new revelations make it impossible to honor this request. Miss Chesterton, please come forward."

Chesterton himself stood in the gallery. "This is preposterous your honor. Sam would never do such a thing. Having known the defendant most of his life, I can vouch for him."

The prosecutor stood. "This happens all too often. Young men in a position of trust begin thinking they deserve more than what is just, and, being denied, force their demands, especially when it comes to matters of a sexual nature. I know you don't want to believe this. That's why your daughter has to testify. She's the only other witness."

Anna stood from her chair, red-rimmed eyes set deep, her face pale. An ageing ghost of herself, she wobbled. Her father hooked his arm in hers and led her to the bailiff, who escorted her to the witness chair.

"Do you swear to tell the truth, the whole truth and nothing but?"

How far will she go with her testimony? Surely, for the sake of her reputation, she won't tell all, but what tributary might she find for escape?

"I do." It came out as a breath.

"Please speak up, Miss Chesterton."

She coughed. "Yes, I do." She sat in the chair, eyes downcast, knotting fingers in the cloth of her skirts.

"Miss Chesterton," said the prosecutor, "Did Sam…"

"No," she said, her voice soft. "No, Sam protected…Sam never…" She looked sideways at Chesterton.

"Did your father warn you against admitting rape?"

219

"My father did not."

"And your aunt? Did she cover this with you?"

Anna squirmed in her seat without answering.

Truth had sat silent on Anna's tongue too long, a toad she swallowed over and over. Sam could see the way her throat constricted. She hadn't the stomach for lies.

To her, a little white lie was a lie, and she refused. Silence was her only refuge. She wouldn't even deflect by answering a different question. Now, silence impossible, Sam knew the truth would spill, and things would get worse.

"I thought so." The prosecutor licked away a satisfied smile.

"She warned me," said Anna. "But I swore...." she looked up, pink circles bright on her cheeks, her eyes sharp. "I swore to tell the truth. And I'm telling...."

Sam groaned. Kane had already named her damaged goods. She mustn't accuse Barth. Kane would add scold to the accusations as punishment for disparaging his son. Auburn and the gag for Anna. Sam couldn't let her do it.

At this point Sam, already bound for prison, only needed to have the charges of rape dismissed. On her feet, "Your honor," she said. "I'm a...."

"No, Sam, it's the only way. Your Honor, if Sam hadn't stopped him...."

Barth shouted from his place at the table, "It wasn't her fault." He jumped onto the chair and beat a righteous fist over his heart. "You can't punish her for Sam's crime." And turning to Anna. "I won't let it happen. I can't let this taint follow you. Anna...."

Imploring, both arms stretched, palms out, beseeching, "I love you. I don't care what people say." His face crumpled as if he might cry, pathetic as a wounded puppy. "Anna, please...." He leapt over the table and onto his knees before the witness chair. Hands clasped as if in churchly prayer, he said loud enough to be heard at the back of the room, "Please, Anna, marry me?"

She blinked. Stunned, a lightning-struck dove, she stared.

The only sound was a soft complaint from her chair as one hand levitated. By slow increments, directionless, it wandered off her lap.

Her lower lip loosened. Pink and vulnerable, it twitched as if to catch elusive words her upper lip couldn't begin to identify.

Her body leaned slightly from the waist, head tilted like a person hard of hearing. One foot shifted to the side of the chair. Her black pupils expanded, deep holes devouring the soft blue iris.

Her wandering hand turned intentional. It rose as she rose to a crouch. Arm stretched, chin forward, she pointed a rigid forefinger at Barth.

A white edge to her pursed lips, they found the word, "You…" Her extended finger shook. "You are the one."

"ANNA!" Chesterton and Sam shouted at the same time. "No!"

"She's right." Barth leapt to his feet. A sudden smile covered his face, the face of a man whose intended had just answered in the affirmative. "I am THE ONE. Yes, *I* am yours."

A low murmur went around the gallery. People shifted in their seats, some concentrating on Anna, others on Barth. They poked each other, frowned. Heads shook no, shook yes. Whispers grew loud.

"That's not what I…." Anna knocked her chair askew. Her finger still pointing at Barth, she twisted toward the judge. "*He* was the one. *He* tried…."

Sam buried her face in her hands. Don't say it… don't say it….

"*His* hands tore my blouse. Those same hands, his, on my breasts, and…."

"And?" The judge said.

"And that's enough," Chesterton shouted from the gallery.

"No, Papa. I promised the truth, and this is true: Sam hit him. Sam stopped Barth before…."

"You claim there was no rape?" said the judge.

"If Sam hadn't stopped him, there would have been."

Rising from his seat, palms down on the table, Kane spoke in a level, commanding tone, "Horace... ah... Your Honor, please. This must stop. Clearly Miss Chesterton has broken under the weight of these proceedings.

"As you've seen, my son has gone above and beyond to rescue her from certain degradation, yet she's turned on him as only a mad creature would.

"Enough now, please. I'm in sympathy with her father. Save her from herself. The truth is obvious, and we needn't carry this charade further. For Anna's sake, please, Your Honor. We're all gentlemen here. Let's behave that way."

The gallery seemed to hold its breath, while the judge ran a hand across his chin.

Mamma stood in the gallery. "Yes, by all means, be gentlemen," she said into the quiet. "But know, my daughter Sam, yes, I say daughter, Samanthos, can't be guilty as accused. For God-sake, she's a girl."

"Madam, *you* are out of order."

CHAPTER 56

OUT OF ORDER

Lungs corroded
Air harsh as water

Or was it Six out of order. Should a sign be hung around her neck. A sign on her numbered door? She was so broken that she wasn't worthy to be numbered, here, living in this step-by-step death.

Middle of the day, the blue above the skylight filled the cell joyless. We hadn't slept. Six coughed deep and wet.

Her own private stream burbled with every breath. "That's right," I encouraged, "cough it up."

"Hur...ts..." She was mid-strangle. Water had closed her pipes, damning her to ongoing hurt.

I stepped over her and climbed off the cot, blanket lifting. Her naked body spasmed, eyes dull under lids at half-mast, skin a cold blue-gray.

Chains had tracked her wrists and ankles, the depressions raw, and with the passage of hours, her joints had swelled. I drew the blanket to her neck and tucked it carefully around her. "You'll make it, Six."

Vomit gushed, mostly water, thank God. I patted her face with my shirttail.

"I'm sorry," I said, knowing the odor of fear.

She put a shaky finger to her lips, eyes sharpening. She breathed, "Ma-ch..."

"The mad chair!" I understood the ever-present threat.

She clutched at the blanket with fingers that wouldn't close, tried to scrunch toward the corner, but like her fingers, her limbs wouldn't do her bidding.

She closed her eyes against me. Held at bay, I waited.

"You have to eat."

She didn't move. I brought cold mush from the slot. She writhed on the cot but couldn't raise herself.

With a hand behind her head, I helped prop her against the wall and offered her a spoonful. Her hands stayed in her lap. She stared at fingers fat as caterpillars on the blanket.

I fed her half a spoonful. The mush sat in her mouth until she coughed it out.

After the first week, the swelling eased, and I was finished with force-feeding. "You look like a corpse," I told her.

I left the food in the slot. "Rouse yourself or a corpse you'll be."

She wouldn't answer, terrified every time I opened my mouth. To quiet me, she oozed from her bed to the floor. Her body, that of another person, she operated as one would a puppet.

On her knees, she fell onto her forearms, head on her hands. Breath shallow and fast, she coughed. Rested. Pushed her right arm ahead, skin grating, and rested again.

The other leg forward, she waited. Gathered herself in illusive wisps, shifted weight to her left side, and pulled forward. The food slot, once claustrophobically close, was now too distant to calculate in miles. And knee to opposite elbow, she plowed on.

CHAPTER 57

DRAWING

Walls a meadow
I lie in the grass
my orchard resurrected

With each day, her joints eased. Though her walk was elephantine, walk she did to the food. Her fingers formed a fist around the spoon.

The sludge in her bowl made her stomach rebel, and with the spoon halfway to her mouth, she flung its contents. Mush spattered the wall. The spatter dripped, lines reminiscent of fall grasses, her fields made manifest spoonful by spoonful, but without trees. She needed trees.

The following day, she staggered into the yard, hand over her eyes, fresh air a blessing she couldn't pull deep into her lungs. She coughed, long and hard. Bent near double, her arms crossed on her chest, she talked in a series of grunts, her tongue flat in her mouth. At first, it took a few seconds to translate; then it came easily, like a second language, the words so like my own, the pain of talk having once been mine.

With a quick hobble, she scavenged the ground, taking a harvest of dead treasures. "Green," she mumbled, and stuffed the few blades of grass in her pants, before scooping dirt into her socks, the bulk of her ankles back to what they'd been, and guarding the spoils. Kin to Quasimodo, she shuffled into the cell. I slid the door shut, not waiting for Ned.

Ned was silent these days. Thinner, always looking over his shoulder. Six, too taken with her trees, wouldn't look him in the eye.

She emptied her gleanings onto the table. "My orchard," she grunted, "I'm coming." With a sharp rock, she drew trees in the mush now dry on the wall, scritch-scritch through to stone, much of the previous mush-made grasses flaking onto the floor.

Trees erect, she scrubbed green across their limbs, scrubbed harder. Grassy juices could only go so far, the stone taking skin instead. Blood dotted the green haze, and she had her cherries.

"Grow," she whispered. Retrieving dirt from her socks, she rubbed at her trees' roots. The dirt fell, too dry to stick.

She cast about. "Earth." She wiped her eyes with a sleeve and turned in a circle. Her arms shot up. "Ah! Brown." Hands clamped on her head, she limped to the in-house.

"No, not that." I caught her arm, swinging her back to her drawing. We struggled. My arms around her, she wilted to the floor, settling amidst the grass, dirt, and dried mush at the base of her tree trunks. I covered her with the blanket. "Sleep," I said, "under the moon." With a rock, I drew a big circle on the whitewash above the orchard.

"No," she said and waved it away.

That glowing orb, once favored, now infused her with rage. Against her stiffness, she rose swift as a cat attacking a roach on the wall. Claws out, she scratched until she snuffed the naked moon the way she'd like to snuff Barth.

Satisfied, she shrank to the floor. I re-wrapped the blanket and, sitting beside her, leaned her against my shoulder. As the evening advanced, dry grass pillowed her head. Stars above dusted the sky.

"Stay the night," she said. "We've scything tomorrow."

CHAPTER 58

LAST OF THE TRIAL

Mamma, out of order! Again, the courtroom erupted, people on their feet craning for a better view of Sam. The judge banged his gavel, banged and banged. "Bailiff, clear the court."

Totally flummoxed, Sam couldn't move as the bailiff and others herded the crowd, all but nipping at Mamma's heels. Chesterton tried to circle back, but a constable with spread arms ushered him out and locked the door. Kane stayed sitting at the table next to Barth and the prosecutor.

No one nipped at him. "Please proceed," Kane said. "I mean, Your Honor, we're ready." The judge frowned, and with a cough, gave the gavel a weak thump.

The prosecutor stood. "Rape is not the charge, Your Honor. Please instruct the jury to disregard any mention.

"I have no more questions for Miss Chesterton. It's clear, as her father said, her health is compromised. In fact, she's compromised to the point of being an unreliable witness and should not continue."

Kane, with an almost imperceptible nod to the judge, turned to the jury. Narrowing his eyes, he scanned their faces and, stopping at each one, jotted two quick words on a piece of paper. Each juror in turn shifted in his seat and looked at his lap.

"The jury will disregard Miss Chesterton's entire statement."

Sam didn't bother listening to the rest. She didn't want to hear the verdict pronounced by the twelve whose names she was sure had been written on Kane's paper, and equally sure he meant them to know it.

The jurors rose and gathered in the corner to the left of the judge. Their whispered deliberation took no time at all, and one imparted a word in the judge's ear. Now sitting straight, not looking at Kane, he announced, "Guilty." He eyed each juror in turn. "So say you all?"

They mumbled agreement and, dismissed, eyes on the floor, they filed out.

CHAPTER 59

THE ORCHARD

Fields a-fire
Charon where are you

The bliss of sleep in her orchard melted, and the next day, out in the yard, Six was the same as a hound left out in the cold for a whole frozen night. Rump on the ground, knees at her chin, she all but yowled at the cell door. She wanted back into the very place she'd been desperate to quit.

Waspish light in her eyes, she bent her head, and unlike a hound, set her spine to the door. She jammed her feet in the stony dirt. She pushed. Her feet slid. She pulled back and pushed again.

"In. Let me in," she cried in the face of a locust advancing across the yard; coming closer, it tilted its big-eyed head. Feelers waved at its newfound meal.

One locust was frightening enough, and this one was followed by many. A plague of them, stick-legged, mandibles gnashing, marched the ground, and from the air a winged cloud dove.

Her feet churned and, reaching behind her, she set her fingernails to clawing the door.

"Six," I scolded, "You just came out." Afraid she'd shriek, I slid the door open and took her hand. She wouldn't have it and crawled over the sill to sit hunched under her trees' protection.

I nestled close amidst her grass, and she pressed her forehead to my shoulder. "The dream," she said, speaking into my shirtsleeve. "It came again."

She'd had it after the trial. In lock-up alone, her companions having been released, sleep took her to the family living room. She piled dried moss layered with twigs, half on the hearth, half on the wide pine boards, and crisscrossed logs on top.

With intent, she lit the moss and blew. Flames caught twigs and snaked into the logs. Before donning bedclothes, she pondered the why. Finding none, she changed her mind.

One at a time with her fingers, she retrieved flaming logs and tossed them into the firebox, but too late; embers had already slipped through the crack between the hearth and the floorboards. Orange glints smoldered in the cobwebs. They dropped flames into the cellar below where she rushed but, in passing the front door, realized that the bolt hadn't been thrown. Distracted from her mission, she slid the bolt into a strike-plate. Missing a screw, it wouldn't hold.

"And the fire?" I asked. "This time, what of your parents?" Outraged, dream or no dream, I bucked her head from my shoulder. "Again, you left them asleep in their beds?"

Six withered, head bent against the trunk of the thickest tree. Not a hanging tree. "To the Styx," she said. "How do I get there?" She folded herself on the wall. "Charon awaits."

"Stop," I hissed. "Together we live, why die now? This isn't the way." I pulled her off the wall.

Agony roaming her eyes, she faced me, the dream all too fresh. "Fire filled the cellar..."

Fire ate the floorboards supporting the weight of chairs and tables, the weight of her parents' bed with them in it, Paul in his; Paul home to do her job, the one he'd been too weak to do in the first place. The three of them—she lived it with them, moment to moment as they felt heat, saw the flame, and with a resounding crack, the floorboards gave. The roar engulfed all as they dropped into the cellar.

"My fault," she said, barely loud enough to hear. "All my fault."

"You know," I squared her shoulders, made her look me in the eye. "*Your* death will destroy them?"

"I'd end their misery. Ned's too."

"You'd compound their misery." I hugged her hard enough to hurt. "We have to get out." I hauled her to her feet. "They may have opened your case."

She sagged in my arms. "I hit Barth, and I'm sorry."

"You can't be sorry." I shook her. "Killing wasn't the point."

"Maybe it was," she said.

"Having wants, that's your guilt. Don't add to it."

"With my death," she said, sly edge to the smallest smile. "Rat-Face hangs."

"Is that what you want, your own petty retribution?" I shoved her against her painted trees. "You'd cut the stalk and leave the root—how can you?"

CHAPTER 60

RELEASE

Oh body
My
body

Outrage unchecked, I bash her forehead with mine. The back of her skull hits the wall, and her legs give. We sink to the floor, blood down the stone.

Mayhem. Blood spreading.

Murder? Have I killed her?

She'd be grateful. But no, she lives.

She must live and with life, her blood and body declare repentance as the founders predicted. Or so they'll claim.

I pull her onto my lap. "Think of Anna." Her head flops. "Don't you die, not now."

So much suffering. Bloody hell, could it be for naught? "Up," I shout and smack her cheek. "Now, or I'm gone."

And leave her to them?

How can I? I believe in her. I do. "Up." On my feet, I pull her arm.

"No more," she says. "Leave me." She's after Charon's hand, not mine, her body limp on the floor.

"You'd accept this certainty, your family left with none?" I dig at places Rat-Face never thought to touch. "And Anna? You'd abandon Anna?"

On her side, she curls into a ball, talking to her knees, "How can I face her? Face them? They burnt in their beds."

"But you didn't." I tip her head. "Look at me. You can't give in."

"I'm a chicken without its head." She closes her eyes. "Dead already. Kane wins."

"No, in living, you win."

"Oh, Willa!" This, a growl, deep in her throat. "I hate you." And hate fills her.

She rises, tall in my face, hands at my throat, and knocks my head as I'd knocked hers, our voices high to the pricked ears of hounds sniffing through the halls, and there's a rap at the door. She freezes.

"Six, my Six, where are you," Rat-Face sneers, sliding the door. "Your time's come." He wants his way, and rags by the in-house long gone, what he wants, he'll take.

CHAPTER 61

WILLA

When Six was Sam, *if she'd listened harder, might she have heard the suck of aphids yellowing fields? Might she have grasped the bite of blood-lusting fleas?*

Could she have fathomed how the mantis munched her husband's head, the slap of his rut uninterrupted as she chewed through his thorax? Her Natural Mother revealed all, and foolish child, did she heed?

No, not a whit—

CHAPTER 62

HIDING

*And heed I must
the will stronger than me*

As the door slides, Six, her eyes more shuttered than shut, melts. I ease her gently to the shadowed floor, and scoot to the cot. Two hands on the metal bar, I slide under.

The door rolls all the way open. Sunlight, sharp behind him, shows only the rat's outline, the hood hanging at his side. His shadow covers Six's body. He laughs. A cur's rumble replaces his funning lilt. "And now…"

He steps inside. Bigger follows.

One sock-covered boot slips on the blood. Rat-Face skids sideways. Sun pours in through the door.

"Ah, crap." A toe to her shoulder, he shifts the body enough to see her blood smeared face. "God damn it."

"Now what?" says Bigger. "You promised."

"Bugger all." The side of his foot to her ribs, Rat-Face rolls her. He kneels beside her, rips open her shirt, puts an ear to her naked chest. "Aaaw, don't do this." His shoulders sag.

Six lies still. Do I hear a snick of pleasure at his fear, the pleasure perhaps keeping her alive? She'll want to see the drowning rat, see him splash. Hear the frantic tread as he….

Another outline leans in the door. "Fergus, what're you doing?" Ned eyes the cornered rat.

"T'wasn't me." Rat-Face shies from the body. "No, no, not me."

"Help!" Ned shouts to the alley. "Get Doc."

A rush outside, and two more pairs of sock-covered boots slide into view. "She's bashed herself," says Rat-Face. He punches Bigger. "Tell them…."

"Hell, wasn't me, neither."

The others laugh. "Sure, sure, tell it to the warden."

Ned kneels beside her. "She needs Doc. Get...."

The others stroll out. "I didn't see nothin', did you?"

Ned leans close. His ear to her breath, on it the words I want her to tell, "Repentance?" Can he hear her, "Or the hand of mayhem?"

Grunting to his feet, Ned pats her shoulder. "I'll get Doc. Warden, too." He rushes for the door. He's not fast enough, and Rat-Face tackles him. "Not Warden." He holds Ned by the knees.

"Let me go." Ned squirms. "I gotta get Doc."

"Say it." Rat-Face twists his short leg. "No Warden."

Wrenching free, Ned delivers a savage kick to the rat's chest. "He'll know it's murder; I don't have to tell." He stumbles to his feet. "Or call it repentance. I could, you know." Ned looms over him. "She goes free, and you, too." With hardly a limp, he runs for the yard. "Repentance or murder, your choice, Fergus."

"Release? No." He chases Ned into the alley. "I'll never be warden."

I crawl from under the cot. "Six, you hear me?" I gather her in my arms. "Don't...Don't let them win." Sweeping loose hair from her face, I wipe blood off her forehead, press my lips to her frown. I rock her.

She gives me a weak smile. "They'll not win." And I see in her eyes a sliver of satisfaction. I see escape; home or across the Stygian River, either way. And in escape, she denies them her fear. Denies them her pain and the pulse of a living body.

They've been the toothsome cat to her mouse long enough. In her denial, supremacy belongs to Six, and she dismantles their mastery. The gag bloodless. The mad chair empty. Her tormentors left flatfooted, shuffling beside their toys.

No more will they leach power from her insignificance. No more making themselves thick with desserts they deem theirs by right.

She'll strip them mousey, their hackles wilting. And curled on the floor, eyes at half-mast, she gnaws the tails they'll whip between their legs, yes. Yes, my Six with the Cheshire grin. Her one sorrow, off to her land or dead, she won't stay to see their insignificance wax.

Until they find another mouse, I want to say, but I'll not dampen her moment.

Though her silence isn't mine, I absorb her grin.

Running feet. We hear them from the alley. "Go," she says. "I pray you." No time to get her to the cot, I hook fingers in the grate and yank, the metal edge cutting as it lifts with a crunch of old mortar.

I, her star-nosed mole in reverse, drop my feet in the long-cooled pipe. Down to my armpits in the hole, I sink the rest of the way, the grate pulled in place above my head.

I worm lower. My foot feels the cross pipe, my path to the furnace, when voices overhead stay me.

"Doc!" It's Ned. "She's alive?"

"You better hope so, at least until her brother gets here."

"How far?"

"Meadowvale? Be here day after tomorrow, he and his wife in a wagon."

I want to tell Six, home's close. Don't give up.

Fight, damn it, the shout in my head loud enough; surely she can hear it. But she weakens, her breath beyond erratic.

So near in the pipe, yet helpless to keep her. I make a fist of fingers that would shove the grate in their faces. I want to lift and carry her home.

Meadowvale. Doc said Meadowvale. Paul with a wife. She would have to be Anna. Wouldn't she? Anna had a soft spot for Paul, so why not?

Had Six known, these happenings could've staunched her flagging hopes. I weep for her. Sam, I call to the person she was, the person full of dreams. She must hear, must know. Sam, don't die now.

To lose her is to lose myself, and I inhale old prayers. It's all I can do—take her hopes and dreams and go forth. And I will.

I'll mole my way into the prison's bowel, my fingers testing for leftover warmth of the shut-down furnace, all the while, bright in my mind, the coal chute, its hatch outlined in light, marking my way.

She sees me go as another person would. But I can't leave her.

CHAPTER 63

FIGHT

Willa's voice so full of homeward promise or is this but another dream prone hour.
Fight. That voice so like Paul. He pleads over the jounce of a square-wheeled wagon, Sam, you have to fight

I can't let her quit, and while we wait for Paul, I force water. Food is not to be managed, but she lives.

Not quite conscious, Six lies on a stretcher, ready for transport. They've washed her and wound a bandage around her head, short hair spiking above and below. They've dressed her in a new white nightshirt fit for a hospital. A thick wool blanket covers her to her chin, her bare feet hardly tenting the end.

I crawl under, too. Enfold her. I hold her, our two gaunt bodies one long lump. Her head is all that shows above the blanket.

We wait.

Through slitted lids I see Ned at one end of the stretcher, Bigger at the other—They joggle our blanketed-bodies down a dim hall. Twists and turns. Rat-Face hustles beside us.

"Is she breathing?" asks Bigger.

"Warden says she better be." Ned steadies the tilting litter. An arm flops off the side.

"We should tie her."

"No time," says Rat-Face. "Go faster." They approach the great oak doors, with a single sliver of light showing down the center. I hear the rusty creak. Six remembers that first suggestion of nightmares to come.

The sliver widens.

"Six, wake up." Rat-Face slaps her cheek. "Say something."

Silence the rule, why break it now? Not with freedom a few feet away. "Come on," he squeaks and, thumb to her eyelid, he pushes it up. Her pupil retreats to its upper reaches, giving him the benefit of a white eyeball. "Ooooh shit."

Six basks in his panic. He could prod out her eye; she wouldn't care. She'd die happy.

"Stop poking," says Ned, fierce. "You've had your fun."

"I'm *not* funning."

The door creaks wider. It's the rat's turn to hear nightmare predictions—murder if she dies. We pass into scalding light.

Songs of finches and sparrows fill my head with remembered summers. I smell greening leaves.

She can't see in the stabbing light, only the outline of a horse and wagon waiting, and two people arm in arm, one short, one tall, a crouch to their knees, wary, as if the mammoth's open mouth would exhale a host of contagion.

Ned and Bigger stop at the wagon. They slide the stretcher, headfirst, over the tailgate and up to the bench ending the long bed. Ned crosses her arm on top of the blanket, and the couple moves in. Their heads block the sun.

Rat-Face is full of unctuous smiles. "Doc says your sister's fine. A bit of a head bump is all. Repentance, really." He slides his palms together. "Right as rain in a few days, you'll see. Doc said she would be." His wheedling rises. "She will. Soon. She will."

I don't move.

"Sam?" The woman's voice. Anna's voice.

"Surely," she says, "this isn't our Sam." She climbs into the wagon.

"'Tis, oh yes," says Rat-Face. He tips her chin, angling her face for a better view. The woman flinches and looks away, as one would from an animal struck down on the road.

He gives Six's cheek an affectionate pat. "So cooperative, a model prisoner."

"There's been some mistake." Anna leans in. She peers. The fingers of both hands go to the corners of her own mouth. They trace her cheeks, smooth where Six's are rutted with jagged lines.

Her fingers shift, hovering above the scars. They curl away, disbelief in the shake of her head, and one finger wanders to the mole on the ridge of Six's ear. The mole, just like mine.

"Look," she says, a quick glance at Paul, and then looks back at Six. "Oh…" Her face is suffused with unspeakable sorrow. "Oh, Sam."

After a swipe at his eyes, Paul vaults to the wagon's seat, almost as lithe as he was before the pox. "We'll…." He coughs, clearing his throat, and gathers the reins. "We'll take you home."

I see the underside of Sam's eyelids, the sun veiled pink. This body belongs to Sam, but I must raise the lids on those eyes— eyes once forced to behold the unendurable.

I feel a lurch. We're moving, and Sam remembers the square-wheeled jolts of the sheriff's cart that brought her. She feels the weight of years on her chest, and I wish her strength enough to draw breath beneath the blanket.

As we wend the cobbles, I watch over our feet. The great stone edifice shrinks into the encroaching city, brick on brick, the houses stuck each to another, overtaking woods and fields.

Cobbles soften to dirt. The land opens to familiar plots of plowed earth ready for planting, and the horse surges homeward.

Anna sits on the bench beside Paul, but faces backward, her elbows on her knees. Plea after plea, soft whispers in Sam's ear, "Sam, come back." All the while, Sam watches clouds scud the blue, not a flicker of the past or future in focus.

"Please, don't go," Anna says. "Our own Little Sam, she's so eager, her brothers, too…they want to meet you." Anna strokes Sam's cheekbone, that one small patch unscathed. "Don't go now. So close to hopeless we'd been, yet here you are."

She leans against Paul, her head on his shoulder. Her words shake. "She can't hear me." Her eyes swim.

Paul twists on the bench. He reaches for Sam and rubs a thumb on the back of her hand. "The kits have come out; only two this year, one with black hackles. Our urchins, they'll show you."

"And Kane's place," Anna says. "Charred bones, that's all that's left."

Paul squeezes Sam's shoulder. "Some semblance of justice. I wish Father had lived to see it. Mamma, too."

By the time we turn at Meadowvale, night has fallen, the sky a spangled arc overhead. Paul brings the wagon to a halt before the porch. Two men emerge and lift the stretcher, carrying it through the entrance and up the grand stairway, past open doors, the children asleep, and into a large room with a four-poster facing a bank of windows.

Sam's bandage changed, her body moved to a soft cloth mattress for the night, Anna kisses her mottled hands—one side and then the other. "You're home," she says.

"And tomorrow...?" She turns to Paul as he raises the sash on window after window.

"We'll see," he says. Anna blows out the lamp, and they head down the hall. The door left open.

From the dark outside, a chorus of peepers sing, their lullaby easing Sam into sleep.

EPILOGUE

The windows wide, I taste advancing spring mixed with the smoke of civil unrest, and in this unsettled world, I pray Sam will keep breathing. Pray she'll keep reaching past the walls of what's allowed. Grasp the improper and makes it hers.

And I will rise if Sam cannot. Annealed in abuse, and honed for the battle ahead, I'll peer behind the shadowed moon. I'll walk the darkest dreams of girls schooled to obedience. I'll echo Sam's small voice in the greatest houses. In humble cottages.

I'll echo her wants in dilapidated shacks, listen anywhere a woman's feet tread the kitchen boards, be they bare feet, feet in silver slippers, or steel-toed boots.

And I promise, though her voice be silenced today, maybe unheard tomorrow, I *will* keep her whisper on the wind.

ಶಿಀ ಶಿಀ

Acknowledgements

Unending thanks to the team at Frayed Edge Press, and especially my editor Alison Lewis for her constant support, understanding, and generosity. She is the best in the business.

And I'm constantly indebted to:

Michelle Hoover and Lisa Borders who, along with my Novel Incubator classmates, helped me open an exciting new world.

To my whole novel group (Nichole Bernier, Kathy Crowley, Juliette Fay, Randy Susan Meyers) for their friendship and laser-like attention to every aspect of this novel and the others I've written.

To my preliminary readers (Priscilla Fales, Belle Brett, Anne Carroll, and the late Gene Brewer) for invaluable feedback; and more to Anne Carroll who started this whole project when she took me, in 2010, to visit the Eastern State Penitentiary. I knew then I wanted to set a story there.

Also to my children, Brad, Cally, and Sarah, and my partner Priscilla, for their love and unwavering belief in me.

And oddly enough, my gratitude extends to my protagonist, Six, who guided me as if holding my hand (along with my partner), diffusing COVID's isolation and the possible ramifications of pancreatic cancer. Six's struggle made me treasure every second of this easy life.

About the Author

E. B. Moore is a metal sculptor turned poet turned novelist. She grew up Quaker in rural Pennsylvania, on a Noah's Ark farm, with two of every animal plus a herd of Cheviot sheep. She raised guinea hens and ring-necked pheasants, and ran a boarding stable, saving her earnings for further education.

E. B. Moore is also the author of the poetry chapbook *New Eden, A Legacy* (Finishing Line Press, 2009) and the novels *Loose in the Bright Fantastic* (Frayed Edge Press, 2023), *An Unseemly Wife* (NAL/Penguin 2014), and *Stones in the Road* (NAL/Penguin/Random House, 2015). She is the mother of three, the grandmother of five, and currently lives with her partner in Scarborough, Maine.

www.ingramcontent.com/pod-product-compliance
Lightning Source LLC
Chambersburg PA
CBHW071515110726
47908CB00003B/843

* 9 7 8 1 6 4 2 5 1 0 6 4 5 *